A
Penchant
for
Poison

A NEVERLAND CHRONICLES SAGA | PART TWO
T.S. Kinley

A Penchant for Poison,
A Neverland Chronicles Saga Part Two
by T. S. Kinley

This is a work of fiction. Names, characters, places, and incidents are either
the product of the author's imagination or are used fictitiously. Any
resemblance to actual persons, living or dead, events, or locales is entirely
coincidental.   ·

First hardcover edition August 2024
ISBN 978-1-964877-02-0

Book design by T.S. Kinley
Editing by Samantha Swart
Cover design by T.S. Kinley
WWW.TSKinleyBooks.com

For those who are still awaiting their happily ever after. Fate always has a plan. Revel in the darkness, so that you will someday know where to shine your light. Your love story will be worth the wait.

AUTHOR'S NOTE

Author's Note
The content in this book contains sexually explicit
depictions. Please be aware of the following possible trigger
warnings and read at your own discretion. Lewd NSFW
depictions of sexual acts, bondage/restraints, BDSM, blood
play, tentacle play, drug and alcohol use, poisoning,
drugging, graphic violence, gore, mutilation of corpses,
hanging, drowning, abduction, assault, guns, swords, hostage
situations, mind control, religion, anxiety, depression, death.

"Who knows the end? What has risen may sink, and what has sunk may rise. Loathsomeness waits and dreams in the deep, and decay spreads over the tottering cities of men."
—H.P. Lovecraft

CHAPTER ONE
-REGRET-
James

This couldn't be happening—not again.

The way Katherine molded her body against Edward's—how she pressed her lips to his—was enough to bring every agonizing memory of betrayal to the surface. I should pick up my dagger and end them both.

And yet, I froze in place as time slowed to a standstill, ensuring I bore witness to my downfall. All at once, the captain's quarters became suffocating. The air was stale and dank. The planked walls of the ship were closing in, trapping me in a nightmare where seconds unfurled into an eternity. Each pulse of my heart was a macabre drumbeat toward my demise. A divine punishment where I lingered in my torment, noting everything in vivid detail.

The slight tremble in her lip.

The sleeve of her shift falling from her shoulder.

The flush of rose on her porcelain skin.

Once upon a time, betrayal ripped out my heart. An event that molded and shaped every hardship I endured. Like a glutton for punishment, I allowed it to happen again. I served her the remnants of my tattered heart on a silver platter, and she devoured me whole.

Regret stuck thick in my throat. I should have killed Edward Teach long ago. It had been some time since I cut ties of loyalty to the man. But the infamous Blackbeard had been my captain, a mentor—dare I say, at times, even a friend. I'd foolishly let my sentiments get the better of me.

But Katherine? Her betrayal blindsided me. Was I truly such a fool? The demon inside me roared, a keening cry for vengeance against this woman. The only person who made me feel something other than all-consuming revenge.

I had always believed it was my fate to deliver vengeance to Peter Pan. But had my hubris blindsided me? Maybe it was my fate to drown in betrayal over and over again.

I should have known the Divine would never let me win. I'd been on the threshold of fulfilling my life's purpose with the object of my heart's desire by my side. But it wasn't to be so—not for a man like me.

Teach pulled away from her, a bewildered expression on his face before he collapsed. The sound of his large body crashing to the floorboards broke my spiraling thoughts. Dragging me back to reality like a violent current. Kat stumbled backward, falling to her backside in a huff.

"It worked," she whispered, gingerly fingering her lips. "It really worked."

"Katherine?"

"We are truly free. The poison—it worked!" she said as her gaze met mine.

"Poison? What poison?"

"It worked," she repeated, her emerald eyes foggy as they drifted back to Teach's limp body sprawled out on the fine rug of the captain's quarters. Images of the kiss they'd shared only moments before cycled through my mind, driving me mad. I couldn't make sense of it all.

My vision flared red as I reached her in two quick strides. I dug my fingers into her arm as I wrenched her from the floor.

"What in the bloody name of the Divine is going on?" I growled.

"I poisoned him. I did it for you."

"How?" The question came out through gritted teeth, barely keeping my temper in check. My love for her was the only thing keeping me from running her through.

"My locket," she said, gently fingering the chain around

her neck. "It contains poison. When I kissed the locket, it transferred to my lips. It was through my kiss that he found his demise." She straightened her shoulders, holding her chin high with her admission.

"Curious, don't you think, that *you* are seemingly unfazed?"

"It was arsenic. I've been dosing myself for years, trying to build an immunity. It affects me, but not enough to kill me." It was then that I realized her words were slightly slurred. I stared at her. Searching her face for the truth. Her pupils were blown out, and she swayed in an effort to remain upright. My hand on her arm was the only thing keeping her on her feet.

"You have to believe me. Please. It was the only way. I couldn't risk you falling to his blade." Tears spilled down her cheeks. The sound of her sobs filled the silence of the cabin. Her tears melted the anger in my chest. The evidence confirming the truth of her story lay at our feet. She had been his victim, even more so than I had. And the Divine had granted her the vengeance she deserved.

"I believe you." She let out a wail, and her body sunk into mine as I folded her into my arms. "Shh… I believe you. I wish you would have told me about the poison, but I believe you. I told you before that I'd be worthy of all your demons, and I'm a man of my word."

I held her for what felt like an eternity. Rocking her on the floor as all the pain she'd endured under Teach poured out of her, dampening my shoulder. I tried to snuff out the jealousy that welled in my gut. Katherine had finally gotten her revenge, while mine lingered like a rotting corpse, deteriorating into something gruesome and unrecognizable. I had to do something soon. I had a date with Peter Pan and my patience was wearing thin.

"Come with me," I said once her sobs had finally subsided. I grabbed her hand, pulling her to her feet.

"What are you—"

"I can't stand to look at him anymore. Let's rid him from our lives once and for all."

She wiped her tear-streaked face with the back of her hand, squared her shoulders, and nodded.

"Can you manage on your own?" I asked, wondering just how much the poison had affected her.

"You still haven't figured out that you don't need to worry about me. Clearly, I can take care of myself," she said, and I didn't miss the accusation in her tone.

"I deserved that," I admitted, shame crawling up from the pit of my stomach. I'd failed to protect her time and time again. She started to walk away from me, a chasm beginning to grow between the two of us, but I'd be damned if Teach would take her from me even in death. I grabbed her arm, pulling her back to face me. "From here on out, I will never let another man lay his hands on you. Not while I'm still breathing. Do you understand me?" My gaze held hers, willing the conviction in my words to leech out of me.

She swallowed hard, her wet lashes blinking as my command settled over her. "Yes, sir." Her tone was submissive but laced with need. She wanted me to take control. Maybe all those years with Teach had warped her mind, but fuck if it didn't have my cock stirring in my pants.

I pulled her hard against me, allowing the notion of her supposed betrayal to heat the blood in my veins. I wanted to claim her, starting with her mouth. I came to my senses a moment before I met her poison-laced lips. My black widow was a dangerous creature, but that only heightened my need for her. I took her neck instead, sucking the delicate skin into my mouth, dragging my teeth over the sensitive spot until she let out a soft moan. My hands roamed down her back, cupping her ample backside and dragging her closer. I ground my now fully hard cock against her and let out a growl of my own. I pulled away from her neck, pleased with the red that bloomed beneath her skin. She was mine, and I wanted to mark her so the entire world would know.

"James, my love, should we—"

"Don't you dare tell me to stop. I've watched Teach put his hands all over you. It's only fitting that he watch me claim you. Even if he is watching from the pits of hell."

Her eyes lit up at my words. She wanted this as much as I did. She was just too ashamed to admit it.

I ripped the soft shift from her body. The sound of the simple cotton tearing filled the quiet space around us. I hummed in appreciation as her breasts heaved, her breath coming in ragged pants. Her delicate pink nipples pebbled in the cool air of the cabin. I leaned down and pulled one into my mouth, desperate to taste more of her. She pressed into me, no longer trying to stop it from happening. I awakened her body, and I wasn't the only one who needed to be sated. I pushed the rest of her ruined shift past her hips, letting it pool on the floor at her feet.

I stepped away from her then. Appraising every inch of the woman to whom I begrudgingly gave a piece of my soul. She was the most beautiful creature I'd ever laid eyes on.

Her thick, golden hair hung in waves over her large breasts, and I pictured just how pretty it would look wrapped around my hand when I sunk my cock into her. She shifted her weight, staring at the floor as she fidgeted with her hands. My intense gaze made her uncomfortable, and the demon in me purred. I enjoyed seeing her flustered over me.

"What are you waiting for?" she finally asked.

"For you to tell me what you want me to do to you."

"What?"

"You've spent years being used. Taken advantage of. But not with me. You deserve to be worshipped. So, tell me what you want. Tell me what you need. Tell me your darkest desires, and I will come crawling at your feet."

She sucked in a breath, a myriad of emotions dancing in her eyes. After a moment's hesitation, she raised her chin. "I want you to take off your clothes. I want to look at you… just as bared as I am."

"Your wish, my sweet girl." A smile crept across my face as I reached for my belt, letting it fall to the floor, pistols and all. I kicked it away from Teach's lifeless body. Old habits die hard. Even in death, the man still seemed strangely dangerous. I made a show of slowly unbuttoning my shirt and unlacing my breeches until I was standing naked for her inspection. She took a hesitant step toward me and traced a trembling hand across my chest and down the lines of my tattoos. Her eyes roamed freely over my body. She struggled with this newfound dominance, and it pulled a smile from the corner of my mouth to watch her.

"And now what?" I prompted. Her gaze flicked to Teach, his still warm body lying just feet away. "Don't look at him. Look at me. What do you want, Katherine?"

"I—I want you to worship me. With your tongue." She said the last part with conviction, and that was all I needed.

She yelped as I grabbed her, pulling her into my arms in a heartbeat and gently laying her on the plush rug. Her body was tense, but she let me spread her thighs wide. Her pretty, pink cunt was dripping for me. The chaos and death that surrounded us was an odd aphrodisiac. I ran my tongue through her wetness. She tasted like sweet victory. We'd overcome all the odds, and now I wanted to revel in the spoils. She moaned, my tongue working over her sex, worshipping her just as she asked. Focusing on the tight bud of pleasure until she was writhing beneath me. The sight of her coming undone was exquisite. I noted all her mews of pleasure, vowing to wipe every thought of Teach from her mind.

"You," I growled, "Will only ever purr for me, Kitten. No one else. This is mine. Do you understand me?"

She nodded her head, another moan escaping her lips, and I pulled away. "I didn't hear you."

"Yes, yes. Please," she panted and bucked her hips in protest to the delayed orgasm.

"Yes, what?"

"Yes, sir. I'm yours. Only yours."

"I knew you were a good girl," I growled before slipping two fingers inside her, hooking them just right. Her body tensed, her walls clenching around me. My name tore from her lips as she climaxed, and a devious smile spread across my face.

"Do you hear that, Blackbeard?" I sneered at the ridiculous nom de guerre he'd earned himself. The infamous beard, now dotted with the white foam that had spilled from his mouth when Kat had poisoned him. "Did you hear her cum for me?" I growled as I grabbed a hold of her hips and flipped her over. I was done being gentle. I couldn't wait any longer. "She's mine now, you bastard!"

I slammed into her from behind, pulling a throaty moan from her as I sheathed my full length inside her warmth. I didn't hesitate, letting my need set a fevered rhythm. My emotions overflowed as I let go of the rage I'd felt when I thought she had betrayed me. My fingers dug into her hips, pulling her into a punishing rhythm, but she met me stroke for stroke. My balls drew in as my climax crested. Her pretty cunt tightening around my cock was my undoing. The sound of our combined moans echoed in the cabin.

I rolled her over, my cock still buried inside her as we lay on the floor, catching our breath. Teach's motionless body in our direct line of sight. The act had been cathartic. We'd hidden our love for too long, and I was done hiding.

It took every bit of my strength to carry Teach's dead weight onto the deck of the ship. I cringed at the sound of his lifeless body slamming against the floorboards. I'm not sure how it was possible to love and despise the man at the same time. I took one last look at him. All the color had drained from his face, his skin looking unnaturally waxy. White foam continued to leak from his mouth, coating his infamous beard. The man would haunt my nightmares for an eternity. With a swift motion, I pulled my dagger from my belt. I wanted to feel my blade split his skin and pour his aubergine blood over my hand, just to prove to myself that he was truly dead.

"James, what are you doing?"

"I have to, Kat. I must know for certain."

"He's dead. It's over. You don't have to do this. You're better than that."

She grabbed my hand, stilling the blade. Her fingers trembled as she wrapped them around mine. All I could see were the horrors that Blackbeard had committed against the both of us, flashing continuously in my mind. I looked into her emerald eyes; they were pleading with me to be done with this man and wash him from our lives forever.

"You're right."

She nodded, and the two of us pushed his limp body over the edge of the ship. I stared at the floorboards rather than watching his body plummet to the watery grave below. The sound of the splash was music to my ears. I was finally free. Teach's death meant the end of a nightmare. It was time to begin a new era. One where I was the master of my destiny. I would never again bow to another's will.

"We should get out of here, Kat. Something about this place feels evil. We need to find the ruby and get to Neverland."

"I found it."

I turned to her, but she continued to stare into the water at what was left of her nightmares.

"You found it? You found the ruby?" My excitement flared at the prospect, but I needed confirmation that she had indeed found the Heart of the Divine before I let it get the better of me. I wasn't sure I could handle the disappointment, not after everything I'd endured.

"That's what I was coming to tell you before…"

She reached into her pocket and produced a ruby that fit neatly in her palm. The contrast of the blood-red gemstone against her porcelain skin was stark. And I remembered the vision she had of me all those years ago.

Blood red.

That is what my future held, and there it was, resting in

her palm—my destiny. The angles were perfectly cut. An ethereal glow emanated from the center as if a specter had taken up residence inside the gemstone.

Gingerly, I plucked it from her hand. The moment it touched my skin, I expected a surge of power to course through me. But there was nothing. The power of the cosmos lay in this simple stone, and it was at my fingertips, begging to be wielded to my whim. But how?

"Do you know how to use it?" I asked, both anxious and hesitant for her answer.

"Are you ready to go back to Neverland, James?"

Chapter Two
-Rules-
Katherine

"You're sure this is it?" James asked, but I couldn't concentrate on his words. My eyes shifted back to the water, fixated on the bubbles rising from the sea as it consumed Edward's body into its depths. Doubt lingered in my mind. I wasn't certain that the poison had truly done its job. I still felt its effects on me, and I'd had years of exposure. But Edward was a large man, and poison was fickle. I hadn't been able to bring myself to check and see if his black heart still beat because my own heart was conflicted. But maybe it had nothing to do with my heart.

All the years I'd been Teach's property had broken something within me. Was I damaged goods? Was my mind so far gone that I could no longer trust myself?

At least I could count on the sea to claim victory over his death if I'd fallen short.

"Kat?" he asked, pulling me from the downward spiral of my thoughts.

"Er… yes. Yes, I'm sure of it. That's the Heart of the Divine." I wrenched my eyes from the sea, determined to put Edward Teach behind me.

"It looks so," his brow creased as he rolled the perfect ruby in his calloused fingers, "unassuming. I mean, it's beautiful. I can tell that it's no ordinary gemstone. But I was expecting something more."

"Can't you feel it?"

"Feel it? It's cold and solid in my hand."

"No, not the tangible. The energy." I paused as he looked at me speculatively. "You do feel it, right?"

How could he not feel the power radiating from the stone? It hummed a haunting call. A sinister whisper that drew me in. This wasn't simply dangerous. It was catastrophic.

"No, I feel nothing. What do you feel?"

"It vibrates with the power it contains. I promise you. This is what you've been searching for."

His face lit with a boyish grin that I'd never seen before. He gripped my shoulders, and the excitement in his forget-me-not blue eyes was infectious. I returned the smile, and he crushed me to his chest.

"There's no time to waste. Neverland has been waiting too long. Now that we have the ruby, how do we use it?"

My heart stuttered, beating erratically in my chest. I told James that the secrets of the ruby would reveal themselves the moment I held it in my hand. I assured him of this. But aside from detecting the vortex of energy that swirled around the stone, the way to harness it remained a mystery to me.

"Well, we should probably get a few things in order before we go. We need to be prepared." I stalled, gnawing on my lower lip as my mind raced. Admitting to him I didn't have the answers I'd promised felt like an utter failure. James had proclaimed his love for me, but a dark part of me whispered that his affections might change if I didn't prove useful.

He nodded absently, toying over my words, his eyes distant and calculating as he stroked his short, sun-bleached beard. "Do you want to see where I found it?"

"Huh, what?"

"Come with me. I should show you what else I found on the ship." I grabbed his large hand and tried my best to pull him to his feet. He didn't move in the slightest, but it was enough to refocus his attention on me. "Come on. You've waited years for Neverland. She can wait a few more minutes. We have our whole lives ahead of us."

This pulled another smile from his lips, and my breath caught in my throat. Paralyzed by the sight of him. He hadn't smiled nearly enough. It was something I would never grow tired of seeing. My future—wrapped in a happy and dangerously handsome package.

"You're right. Show me what new mysteries you've uncovered."

I GRIPPED a polished silver candelabra tightly, hoping James wouldn't notice my hand shaking as I led him into the bowels of the ship. My mind was reeling, trying to determine how I could make the ruby work for him. But the harder I concentrated, the further away the answers seemed to be.

I pushed the nagging thoughts from my mind and focused on the task at hand. We followed the same path I'd taken earlier while searching for food. A gnawing in my stomach and the promise of an evening reveling in our newfound freedom had been more than enough incentive to scour the ship. But now that seemed like a lifetime ago.

We approached the familiar door, another piece of the puzzle waiting just behind it. Years of neglect had rusted the hinges, making it nearly impossible for my slight frame to open. I pushed my shoulder against the solid wood and with a groan, it gave way.

Candlelight illuminated the grim scene as the musty scent hit me. It was a peculiar smell—one of decay that lingered in the air, even though the men who sat around the center table had been long since dead. It was an echo of the stench that must have once filled this room.

The three of them were little more than parched skin pulled tight over their skeletal remains. A moment frozen in time. As though they'd been in casual conversation when their souls were ripped from their bodies.

"Did you find yourself in Davy Jones' locker?" James breathed, his cunning eyes taking in the small room. It was starkly appointed, the only furniture being the table and chairs. There weren't portholes this far below deck, and the dark wood paneling gave the feel of a cave.

More curious than the dead pirates were the rubies that covered the table they sat around. Each one was a perfect replica of the Heart of the Divine that James now clutched in his hand. Their identical cores swirled with a specter of false magic. The convincing decoys were nothing more than pretty paperweights used to disguise the true ruby.

"Do these stones speak to you, too?"

"No. These are all fakes. If you cannot feel the vibration of power in the true ruby, then you would never be able to tell one from the other."

"Manann, you tricky bastard." James walked around the table, fingering the maps and books that lay strewn amongst the gemstones. "This looks like the captain's log," he said, fingering the frail, discolored pages of a leather-bound book.

Journal of the voyage, by Divine permission, in the good ship, Jolly Roger, entered by acting Captain Starkey, as our prior captain hath succumbed to the beasts that lurk in the deep. This may well be my last entry as we have depleted the food stores. There are but three of us left out of the crew of two hundred. These are dismal odds, and we are no closer to finding the Heart of the Divine than we were the day we set sail from the safe harbors of Patreyus.

We were once proud fae of the first realm, but now we toil in this otherworldly place that teeters on the ley lines. All the while, piles of rubies mock us. If only the Captain hadn't been such a cynical prick and had confided the true nature of the stone to at least one of us, maybe we wouldn't be starving with our salvation hiding right before our very eyes. The quest is all but lost. Signing off for what may be the last time, may the Divine have mercy on our souls.

JAMES READ THE PASSAGE ALOUD, shedding light on the mystery of this ship and those who inhabited it. Now, there was no question; the *Jolly Roger*, as they'd called it, was not of this realm. I stared at the skeletal remains in awe, feeling very small in their presence, wondering what they had seen throughout their lives.

"You truly are a magnificent thing, Katherine," James started, breaking the spell and bringing me back to reality. "These fae, even with all of their magic, couldn't determine which stone would save them. And you, a mere mortal, were able to see it instantly. You truly are my diamond in the rough... or should I say, ruby?"

I blushed fiercely under his praise, but it wilted quickly. I wanted nothing more than to please him. My inability to tap into the power of the ruby nagged at me. What would he think of me when I confessed the truth of my inadequacies? My anxiety unfurled in my chest and tightened around my fundamentally defective heart.

"Thank you," I whispered as he looked at me expectantly.

"It's such a shame that we'll have to leave the ship behind, but it would be an impossible feat," he continued, idly tossing our ruby and catching it in his fist. Casually holding a world of power in his hands. "If only we had a few more men to put her out to sea. She'd make a mighty fierce presence in Neverland." The words no sooner left his lips than those sinister whispers became a roar in my head.

I pressed my fingers into my temples. The noise filled my ears with chaos for a moment, and then—deafening silence. I peered up at James to see if he'd heard it too, but he seemed oblivious, fixated on the ruby as if staring at it would unlock its secrets.

I jumped when a clacking filled the space, and this time, James heard it, too. Both of us tensed at the sound. My eyes caught on the corpse nearest me and watched in abject horror as his dangling jawbone became animated. It rose from where it had fallen on the dead man's chest and clicked back into place. James pulled his cutlass, grabbed my arm, and tucked me behind him. I peered out from behind him, unable to look away. The click and pop of bones realigning was a sickening sound. The sunken, discolored skin of the corpses rejuvenated, their bodies returning to the vigor of life before our eyes.

The corpse across the table pulled in a deep, wheezing breath, exhaling a plume of dust before his eyelids popped open. I had to remind myself to breathe as intelligent, amber eyes regarded me from across the room.

"You can put that down now, boy. You have nothing to fear from us," the fae said, his voice a rich, sophisticated baritone. With his grey-streaked hair neatly pulled back, he exuded an air of refinement that was only enhanced by his well-tailored clothes. He looked more like a gentleman than a pirate.

"I think that's quite unlikely," James replied.

The man chuckled to himself, rubbing the bridge of his nose. The other two corpses pulled in the same wheezing breath, and suddenly, James and I were outnumbered. "Looks like not much has changed, boys. Pirates are still a suspicious lot," he said to the others.

"I'd like to think of it as good prudence," James responded.

"Aye, that's just semantics."

"Possibly. But might I point out that it was you who was

dead only moments ago while I've been very much alive and would like to continue being so."

The fae nodded his head at James before pushing back from his chair.

"The name's Montgomery Starkey, or simply Starkey. I am but a humble school usher turned pirate. But of course, all the good fae are, aren't they?" He raised an eyebrow at James, who still held his cutlass poised for battle. "This is Cecco, and Mason—Alf Mason. We are at your service, Captain." Starkey bowed gracefully, holding the pose while he waited for James to acknowledge him.

The other two glared at us across his bowed back. They were a little less refined. The fae closest to me—the one he called Cecco—leisurely pulled a rusted knife from his belt and began picking at his teeth. His earlobes had been stretched and filled with gold pieces of eight that reflected in the candlelight. While Mason peered out from under his tricorn hat at us, his gaunt face cast in shadows.

"Captain?" James questioned. Both of us still trying to decipher what was going on here.

The fae all chuckled as if they were in on some kind of joke.

"Did you not summon us from our eternal sleep? Did you not call upon the Heart of the Divine to fulfill your need?"

"I… I'm not sure."

Starkey shook his head. "And to think we toiled our lives away looking for the ruby, and it finds itself in the hands of a man who doesn't even realize what he possesses."

"We know full well what it is," I snapped, jumping to James' defense before I thought better of it.

"A fiery little lassie you've got," Cecco said, his graveled voice raising the hairs on the back of my neck.

"The *lassie* is none of your concern," James growled, setting his sinister glare on the fae. "But you're right in one respect, Mr. Starkey. I control the ruby, which makes me the Captain by Divine right." James straightened his shoulders, shedding his earlier hesitation, and stepped easily into the role of authority. The tone of his voice demanded allegiance.

"There are a few ground rules to discuss," Starkey said.

"Ground rules? I have the ruby; I make the rules."

"If only it were that simple. I'm sure you've heard the saying 'with great power comes great responsibility'? We were brought back to serve your needs, but we've been tasked with bringing you a message directly from the Divine."

James eyed him skeptically. But they'd been in the other world only moments before, so I guess anything was possible.

An all-encompassing light enveloped the fae for a moment and then subsided, leaving tracks in my vision where the light had been. When I focused on the reanimated pirate, his eyes glowed, his irises now a swirling, milky white.

"Hello, James," an ethereal, androgynous voice replaced Starkey's deep baritone. My eyes darted to James. He was clearly shaken as the fae... thing... addressed him directly. "If you are to wield the ruby, you must heed these warnings.

"One. The ruby cannot be used to alter the course of destiny or bring harm to the innocent.

"Two. The ruby operates on the principle of balance. An equal consequence elsewhere in your life will offset any benefits gained from its power threefold.

"Three. The ruby is not bound to any being, mortal or immortal, and may choose to depart from its wielder if you're deemed unworthy or its purpose has been fulfilled.

"Do you understand and accept the weight of this obligation?"

"I...uh, yes, ma'am. I mean, sir... Your Holiness," James said, fumbling with his words.

Starkey's eyes shifted back to a dark brown. "Please, Captain," Starkey said, this time in his own voice. "We are here to serve. Do you have our bearings?"

James stared at him for a long moment before shaking his head. "Thank you, Mr. Starkey... for the message. Next time, how about a bit of warning if you're planning to invoke the Divine?" Starkey stared with his arms crossed behind his back, patiently waiting for orders. "Right. Now that we've got that straight, tell me, are there more of you? Might be hard-pressed to navigate this ship out of here with only the four of us."

"The crew will have been long since swept away through the portal. We are the last three to remain on the ship."

"Portal?" James asked.

Starkey gazed questioningly at his companions, who stood stoic, silently appraising the situation. "Last we knew, the *Jolly Roger* sat in the belly of a mountain. Did you not wonder how she came to be there?"

James remained silent for a moment, pondering the question before he answered. "We've only just arrived. The ruby was our first priority. You graced us with your presence just as we were formulating a plan. But tell me more."

"A slip in time. A wormhole. A void between realms if you would. It took us centuries to find. Who knew the gods would hide such a valuable treasure in such an insignificant realm? But I digress. With that ruby, the portal can bring us anywhere in the cosmos."

"But how does the stone work, exactly?" James asked.

"You only have to focus on your intentions. Set your mind to your wants and desires and speak the words to life."

A well of excitement built in my chest, cutting through the knot of anxiety. This stranger had saved me from revealing my failures to James. It all made sense now. When James had wished for a crew, the ruby had manifested it into reality.

"That's it?" James sounded incredulous as he scratched at his beard, obviously not convinced that Starkey had all the answers. "The most complex magic in the universe, and all I have to do is think about what I want?"

"There is beauty in simplicity, is there not?" Starkey said.

"Or destruction," he countered. "The Heart of the Divine in the wrong hands would be a nightmare."

Starkey eyed James thoroughly. "That remains to be seen, Captain."

James growled at the veiled appraisal of his character before ending the conversation with a clipped order. "I suggest you get topside and make yourself useful. I want her ready to sail. We have our heading."

The fae filtered past us without another word.

"James," I said, holding him back from following our newfound crew. "Are you sure we can trust them?" I whispered.

"They owe their very existence to me, and with this," he grasped the ruby tight in his fist, "I could take that all away. I think that is enough to keep them loyal," he reassured me. "Come on. Our destiny awaits." He placed a solid kiss on my temple and pulled me toward the main deck.

CHAPTER THREE

-HOME-

James

Neverland... Peter Pan... Revenge. Neverland... Peter Pan... Revenge... The words cycled through my mind. I closed my eyes and envisioned myself walking along her rocky shores, Peter in a bloody heap behind me. My heart pounded as the wind began to stir the air around us.

"James, it's working. Look." Katherine grabbed my hand, gripping it tightly.

I tried to quell my excitement. Focus, damn it. *Neverland, Peter Pan, revenge. Neverland, Peter Pan, revenge.*

The surrounding water swirled up into a giant

maelstrom, aimlessly tossing the ship about like a fallen leaf caught in the wind. With the ruby firmly gripped in my palm, I locked my arms around Kat, trapping her between myself and the mainmast. We were too close to lose now. I wouldn't allow the growing chaos to tear us from the ship.

Walls of water surrounded us on all sides while an unseen force pulled the ship deeper into the murky depths. Anxious energy coursed through my limbs while my heart pounded against my ribs. Had we made a mistake? Had my obsession gone too far? Had I allowed it to burn too hot? Darkness descended upon us, shrouding us in pitch-black nothingness. The *Jolly Roger* lurched violently onto its port side, rolling itself over completely moments before shooting up through the vortex of water.

Light spilled over us with calm skies once again above our heads. As quickly as it had begun, it seemed to come to an abrupt end as the ship bobbed calmly along the surface of the water once again.

"Are you okay?" I reached up, brushing the mussed hair from Katherine's beautiful face. She had been in my arms the entire time we 'traveled,' but I couldn't be too sure. We had no idea what the cost of using the ruby was or what consequences we would face, if any at all.

Kat reached up, grabbed my face and kissed me gently. "I'm fine, James." She smiled before looking around. "Did it work? Are we back in Neverland?"

Gathering my bearings, I scanned the horizon. Off in the distance, shrouded in storm clouds, was the familiar profile of my beloved island. Either Peter was in a mood, or the island knew I was here to take my revenge. An ominous warning to the natives of the dark days ahead. My heart pounded with excitement, and a wicked grin spread across my face. All my sacrifices, suffering, and relentless desire to return to Pan had finally paid off. Neverland and all her splendors were mere moments away. Peter was about to taste my wrath.

"At last!" I jumped into the air, pounding my fist at the sky before kissing the ruby. "Ha ha! Yes, we did it!" Reaching for her face, I pulled her in for another kiss. "We did it, Katherine." I picked her up and spun her around in my excitement. "Thank you for finding the Heart of the Divine. This wouldn't be happening if it weren't for you."

"I do believe, Mr. James, that *this* was all you." Katherine's words warmed my heart. It had nearly cost me my life to get back to Neverland, but it had been worth it. Now, the real adventure was about to begin.

"Starkey! Hoist the sails and prepare the ship. We set sail immediately."

"Aye, aye, Captain. Crew, you heard him. Make haste."

"Miss Hawkins," I said playfully, matching her flirtatious use of my formal name. "Join me in the captain's quarters. While the crew mans the ship, I'll draw a map to help you find your bearings."

I clutched Katherine's hand as I dragged her to our cabin, barely able to contain my excitement. In all its fine velvets, the room felt suffocatingly small with the entirety of

Neverland waiting just beyond the walls. I searched the cluttered table in the center of the room, my eyes landing on an old map. "This will suffice." I flipped it over and quickly sketched out the island, dividing the land into its regions. "We'll set anchor here—Three Pence Bay. It keeps us fairly close to the Lost Boy's camp and provides us with the cover of the Viridianwood. It's unlikely Princess Tiger Lily's sentries will be actively patrolling this area of the island."

"Princess Tiger Lily?" Katherine asked, her eyes widening.

"I'll tell you more about her in a moment. I want to keep our arrival a secret for as long as possible. Finding Pan will be easier if he doesn't know we're lurking in the shadows."

She nodded, focusing intently on every word.

"The Mysterious River leads you into the island, keeping the Viridianwood to your left. Just beyond the end of the river, due east, you'll find the Lost Boy's camp."

"That's where Pan will be?"

I huffed. "Pan likes to wander the island alone. He's rarely ever at home."

"Hmm, that's going to make it more complicated."

I chuckled. "Nothing good comes easy."

"We have the ruby. Maybe we could use it to locate him?"

"It is tempting." I pondered the idea. With no solid information on the cost incurred from using the relic, I decided it wasn't worth the risk. "I feel it is best to avoid any ill consequences at this time. The island is small. We'll find him," I said, gently dismissing her suggestion, and continued my summary of the regions. "Northwest of the Mermaid Lagoon and due north of the Viridianwood is Tiger Lily's village."

"The Princess?"

"Yes, Neverland is governed by fae. Tiger Lily comes from a line of Divine Chosen. She is a nymph—native to the island. Much like Pan, she looks considerably younger than her years."

"How young?"

"Adolescent."

"And she's the ruler here?"

"Well, technically, her father is, but more often than not, he's gallivanting around the realms on diplomatic missions, leaving Tiger Lily to rule in his stead. But don't let her youthful appearance fool you. She is a powerful force to be reckoned with. Her people age extremely slowly, even by Neverland's standards. Time here moves at a snail's pace."

"Captain," Starkey popped his head into the doorframe. "We have arrived and dropped anchor. The rain appears to be passing."

"Perfect. Prepare to go ashore."

"KATHERINE, WELCOME TO OUR NEW HOME." I ushered her delicate frame over the rocky shores. "Watch your step. The rain has let up, but the rocks will be slippery."

"It's beautiful!" she gasped. "More so than I could have ever imagined."

Neverland welcomed us with its picturesque landscape. The smooth grey stones of the shoreline gave way to the lush, vivid greens of the Viridianwood. The sun peeked out from the clouds, casting glimmers of sparkling light along the surface of the Mysterious River.

"Please allow me the honor of showing you around. We will start our tour along the banks of the river and continue northeast around the island."

Going straight up the river to Tiger Lily's village would have made more sense, but curiosity was eating me alive. I had to get eyes on Pan. The sooner, the better. Heading northeast would ensure we would find ourselves within the outskirts of the Lost Boy's camp, and I could use the Mermaid's Lagoon as a diversion.

"Shouldn't we head into the forest?" she asked. "We need to find food and supplies."

"The Viridianwood is an extremely dangerous place, Kat. Evil lurks between the trees. We'll be better off taking our chances along the banks of the river." She looked at me with suspicion. Her eyebrows raised in question.

"Are you sure you're not just taking us straight to the Lost Boy's camp?" She grinned. "Maybe you shouldn't have drawn me a map? Your vendetta against Pan can wait. We need rations."

"My love, I'm simply taking you to see Neverland's best. Don't you want to see the Mermaid's Lagoon? I'll send the crew out for rations while we explore."

Katherine rolled her eyes. "You underestimate me, James.

I can see right through your schemes. You'd be wise to remember who I am."

"Starkey," I ignored her retort, "appease Miss Hawkins. You, Cecco, and Mason head into the forest. Find us a beast for dinner. Better yet, make it two."

"Aye, Captain."

"We'll return to the ship later this evening. Have something ready for a celebratory feast. We have much to be grateful for."

"Thank you," Katherine whispered, placing a chaste kiss on my cheek. "Now, show me this magical lagoon."

THE ISLAND SEEMED SMALLER than I remembered. The Mysterious River was massive in my mind's eye. Crossing it would have been a grand feat. Something to brag about to the other Lost Boys. Today, it seemed all too mundane. Completely average in every way.

In my naïve youth, Neverland was an endless, magical realm of wonder and amusement. Excitement waited around every corner. There was a dullness to it now. As though my years had sullied its perfection, somehow exposing the truth behind the magic. One thing remained the same. Danger still lurked within the shadows, and I wouldn't stay hidden for long.

I had hoped to catch a glimpse of Pan on our way to the

lagoon. Sadly, nothing stirred apart from the never-ending tinkling of faerie chatter. I listened closely, hoping to overhear any mention of Peter, yet the forest continued to veil his whereabouts.

"Are you ready to see the lagoon?" I asked as the whooshing sound of the waterfall grew louder around us. "How are you with heights?" I chuckled, remembering the ten-foot drop just ahead.

"Heights?" Katherine stopped moving as her face paled.

I toed the edge of the cliff face, knocking down a few small rocks. "Don't worry, you can do this." I jumped down with ease and reached my arms up to catch her.

"I'm a little worried about seeing mermaids again. The last time wasn't so… enchanting," she confessed, hesitating at the edge.

"Come on, jump."

Kat sighed, sitting on the edge before scooching off into my welcoming arms. Her delicious curves slid along my body, igniting a fire within.

"Nothing to worry about, love. You're safe with me. If one of them tries to lay a slimy finger on you, we'll be having sushi for lunch."

"I like fish," she smirked, reaching up on her tiptoes, pausing a mere breath away from kissing my lips. "Catch me."

Kat turned and darted off down the path towards the water's edge. I immediately gave chase, sprinting after her.

Heading straight for her hips, I tossed her over my shoulder, kicking and screaming.

"James!" she squealed. "Put me down."

"Oh no, little kitty Kat. You started this when you chose to run. I caught you fair and square. I *will* have my way with you." I slapped her ample ass, eliciting another satisfying squeal. "You can explore the lagoon when I'm done with you." I circled the water's edge and headed straight for the cliff wall.

THE GROTTO WAS JUST as beautiful as I remembered. Maybe there *was still* some magic here in Neverland. The cavern opened up to reveal a large turquoise pool. A single ray of light cascaded down from a small opening in the glittering ceiling, illuminating the water with an ethereal glow. Crystalline stalactites mimicked the night sky in a vain attempt to outshine the stars.

Holding her arms firmly above her head, I pinned Kat against the wall and claimed her delicate lips with my own. I kissed her as if it were our last, taking my time and savoring the delectable taste.

"Is this what you wanted, kitten?" I asked, placing kisses along her neck. Her breath hitched as I nipped along the curve, making my way to her shoulder. I pulled in a deep breath, savoring her intoxicating scent. She had known telling me to chase her would trigger my baser instincts. She was betting on it. "Did you want me to hurt you?" I growled, pressing my body against hers, ensuring she knew how excited I was.

I didn't wait for her to answer. I spun her around, making quick work of her laces. I wanted her naked—now. Her dress slid effortlessly down her smooth shoulders and past her hips. I let it pool on the ground before slapping her ass. A beautiful pink bloomed under my hand. "You like it rough, don't you?"

"Yes," she mewed, pushing her ass back against me. "Make it hurt."

"Hands against the wall," I ordered, taking a step back to admire the view. Her porcelain skin appeared luminescent in the dark cavern. Her generous curves were highlighted against the sparkling wall like a gift from the gods. I slid my hands up her belly, grasped her breasts, and pinched her pebbled nipples hard, drawing out a startled moan. "I'm going to make you purr." Dropping my breeches, I slid my cock through her cheeks, finding her ready and wanting. "Such a good girl, so wet for me."

"Please," she cried out, pushing back against me. "I need to feel you inside me. Please!"

Who was I to keep my lady waiting? I grabbed her hips and thrust myself deep into her core, groaning at the overwhelming sensation of her tight, little pussy stretching to accommodate my length. I wouldn't last long. Her body was made for me. Every move had me seeking more. I pulled out and slammed back in, sinking myself to the root. "I'm going to make you cum while I'm deep inside you, and then, when you are spent, I'm going to use you for my own pleasure." I knew the words would trigger her, but deep down, she liked it.

"Yes, Captain," her voice was meek and laden with want.

My hands slid down her soft belly, making my way to her clit. I memorized every silky inch of her skin, thanking the Divine for giving me such a perfect woman. Her pussy gripped my cock with my touch before opening up to take more of me. "That's my good girl; take every inch of me," I praised. Slowly, I stroked her while remaining still sheathed inside. Her breath quickened as she moaned with each stroke.

"More," she begged.

I sped up my rhythm, and without warning, Katherine cried out. Her pussy pulsing around my cock. "Fuucck, kitten, cum for me." The sensation of her orgasm gripping tight against me almost pushed me over the edge. I allowed her to ride out her pleasure, stroking her swollen clit until her insides relaxed and her wetness seeped out along my shaft. "My turn."

I gripped her hips and began thrusting at a punishing pace.

"James!" she cried out. The sound of her voice threw me into an animalistic frenzy. Ecstasy ripped through my body. I lost all control and spilled my seed deep within her. This woman had me in a daze. I pulled out and quickly dropped to my knees. Her beautiful slit was glistening with our love. I reached up, gathering the leaking cum with my fingers, and pushed it back inside. "We taste delectable together," I groaned, licking my slick fingers.

I arranged our discarded clothing into a makeshift nest, gently pulling Katherine down to the floor and tucking her into the crook of my arm. "I'll never tire of pleasuring you." It was true. Making Katherine purr brought me a pleasure like no other. She smiled as I nestled my face into her hair. "Watching you lost in bliss is a Divine gift."

Her fingers lazily traced along my shoulders, sending shivers through my body. "You, James, are the Divine gift. I thank the stars every day for crossing our paths."

I paused at her words. Without Katherine, I never would have known love. She was a glimmering ray of light in my darkness. A beacon guiding me to my destiny. I owed the fates my gratitude, yet my mind found a way to slink back into the negative. "I fear the island will take our memories, and I'll forget how much I've enjoyed watching you over the years. The first time I saw your naked perfection," I groaned, remembering just how enticing she was in Teach's tub that night on the *Queen Anne*. "How I longed to worship at your feet."

She giggled at my compliment while a surge of blush spread across her cheeks. "James, that will never happen. Why would you forget?"

"Oh, but, kitten, it will; it's only a matter of time."

Kat looked up at me, her brows furrowed in question.

"For all of its beauty, Neverland has its shortcomings. Time on the island moves much slower than you're used to.

A single day here can equal many days, if not weeks, back in our realm. Along with that, your memories will fade much faster. Your trials with Blackbeard, your parents, and society's misgivings against you will all soon be gone from your mind."

"How is that possible?"

"How is anything on this island possible? It just is. You'll go mad trying to figure out the enigma that is Neverland. Best to just accept it as it is and move on." I reached for her face, searching her worrisome eyes. "Fear not, my dear. Our love is transcendent." I gently kissed her soft lips, sealing them with a promise. "We will stand the test of time. You are mine, and I am yours. Neverland can have my memories. My heart—belongs to you."

"I could never forget you, James. I won't allow the island to take that from me." She placed a chaste kiss on my lips before quickly changing the subject. "Shall we go looking for mermaids?"

"That was the plan until you decided to run. Let's go," I sighed. "I'm eager to see the joy on your face when you see the magic of the lagoon."

CHAPTER FOUR
-LOYALTIES-

James

Watching Katherine enjoy the mermaids warmed my cold-blooded heart. I was starting to believe we could actually be happy here in Neverland, even build a home of our own. I smiled at the thought of it. Kat seemed enthralled with the enchanting beauty of the island. Everything was falling into place. Maybe I would get my own happily ever after, after all. If only I could get eyes on Pan.

Peter had always been abreast of everything going on in Neverland. Why was my arrival any different? Surely, someone had spotted us by now. It wasn't every day that a massive three-masted pirate ship anchored off the coastline. Yet nary a Lost Boy in sight. No telltale crowing, nothing. The anticipation was killing me. All these years—*waiting*. Was it too much to ask that the Divine give me a mere glimpse of the boy? It would be dark soon, and I was desperate for a taste, drowning in my obsession. I purposefully lingered within the outskirts of the Lost Boy's camp, pointing out the hollowed-out trees that were chutes to the underground caverns Peter forced us to live in.

"You lived underground?" she questioned, squinting her eyes.

"Unfortunately—yes. It was utterly miserable, dark, damp, and earthy." I shuttered, remembering the smell.

"And you got in through the trees? But...How?" She looked even more confused. "Wasn't it tight...inside the tree? Did anyone ever get stuck?"

"We each had our own tree. And if you didn't fit, Peter— would do things to you...to make you fit."

"He would do things to you?" She pondered. "What kinds of things?"

"I'll spare you the horrors. You don't want to know. Let's just say, once you fit, you'd do anything in your power to keep fitting."

"The more I learn about this, Peter, the more I don't like him."

I'd never tire of hearing her say those words. Her validation had my demon purring with delight.

We fell into a companionable silence as we walked. My eyes constantly scanned the surrounding forest for any sign of Pan, purposefully stopping at places I remembered from my youth. So many things had changed over the years.

We stumbled across a small, run-down pixie colony. A few empty lanterns hung haphazardly from the branches of a large oak tree. And where there were lanterns, there were pixies. "Do you know what these are?" I asked, pulling one down.

Katherine shrugged her shoulders. "A lantern?"

"This is a *faerie lantern*. Pixies often use them as their homes. Lucky for us, this one appears to be vacant."

"Does that mean pixies live in the area?" she asked, a smile spreading across her face.

"Shhh!" I looked at Kat and pointed just ahead. "There's one now."

She sat on a low-hanging branch, facing away from us, lost in her own company. Clearly, this was a gift from the Divine. It was too easy. I snuck up behind her and snatched her in my fist.

"James!" Katherine gasped. The smile was instantly gone from her face. "What are you doing?" Her brow furrowed, and anger bloomed in her stare.

"It's just a pixie, relax. Haven't you ever caught fireflies in a jar? It's no different. It'll be dark soon. We need her for light—and faerie dust." I shoved the unsuspecting faerie into the lantern. A myriad of furious tinkling bells filled the air, and her voluptuous, luminescent form shifted to a bright red. I lifted the lantern, making eye contact with the little creature inside. "I suggest you change your attitude, or I'll change it for you." The little pixie huffed, slamming her fists at her sides. She took a defeated breath and paled to a brilliant golden light. "That's better. Look at how pretty she is." I smiled, staring at my curvy specimen.

"What the fuck, James?"

I refocused my attention on Kat. She was now the one seeing red. "Katherine," I sighed. "You can't be serious."

"You cannot just hold her captive," she pleaded. "What's next? Are you going to come up with some perverted use for her, too?"

"I have no need to molest the pixie. Unless, of course, *you* want to bring her into our bed." The idea alone had my mind whirling. "They *can shift* to human size if they want to. As for keeping her captive, I can, and we will."

My words only fueled her anger more. "I will not—"

"Katherine," I interrupted her tirade. "She is unharmed. We need her."

"I can't allow you to do that to her, James. After everything I went through. Everything Blackbeard did to me, I would hope *you*, of all people, would understand. I know what it's like to be held against your will. We can't. I won't."

"Katherine, sweetheart, I understand your plight, but we are in Neverland. It will be dark soon, and we still have to pass the outskirts of the Viridianwood." I tried to reason with her. "The beasts will be hunting for their dinner, and I don't want to end this perfect day by digesting in their bellies."

"You will release her when we get to the ship." Her words were an order.

I chuckled condescendingly. "It's not up for discussion. We need her. I give you my word; she will be treated with kindness."

"Jas? Is that you?" A confused, masculine voice called out from amongst the trees. Blissfully ending the argument with Kat and stopping me dead in my tracks.

"Who said that?" I drew my sword and shoved the faerie lantern at Kat for safekeeping. I scanned the surrounding landscape, but nothing moved. The number of beings left in Neverland who would remember me was slim. And the voice was too mature to be Peter.

"It can't be?" The voice was a whisper this time.

"Be a man, and show yourself, coward."

I heard the forest floor rustle before I saw a familiar face emerge from the trees. Dain had an otherworldly beauty that was hard to forget. He had been training as one of Tiger Lily's sentries when I was taken back across the veil.

"I am no coward. Identify yourself," he said, his face contorted with bewilderment.

"Dain, it is I, Jas."

A look of shock flitted across his amber eyes. I assumed the fae were well aware that once a Lost Boy disappeared, they were quickly forgotten, never to be seen again. "You have changed, old friend, or should I say—grew up?"

"Aye, It's Captain James now." His choice of words was not lost on me. I *had grown* up, while many others like me never got the chance. I was not the boy he once knew. "Tell me, what brings you to this part of the island?"

"You tell me, *Captain James*," his voice was full of sarcasm. "Why are *you back* in Neverland? And who is this beautiful creature hiding behind you?"

"She is none of your concern. I'm here to pay Pan a visit. It's been far too long, don't you agree?"

He stared at me for a long moment. I could see the wheels turning as he took measure of me. "Is that your ship anchored out in Three Pence Bay?" he asked, redirecting the conversation that was beginning to feel more like an interrogation.

"Aye."

"I'm on reconnaissance for Princess Tiger Lily. There have been reports of a rogue band of Lost Boys roaming the Viridianwood. The village is on edge, and your ship's arrival was enough to launch an official investigation. You wouldn't know anything about that, would you, *Lost Boy*?"

"I'm no Lost Boy, Dain." I spat the words.

"Once a Lost Boy, always a Lost Boy."

"Those days are long over. Peter exiled me, remember?" I paused, giving him a moment to search for the details that likely wouldn't surface. "I'm sure it's hard to keep track when Pan thins out his ranks so frequently," I added when all he produced was a confused look. "It was my crew hunting for dinner in the Viridianwood earlier today. Consider your mystery solved."

"Unless your crew was here days before your ship, your *men are* not the rogue Lost Boys we are looking for."

My blood began to boil. Only now that these forsaken Lost Boys were deemed a possible threat were the fae getting involved.

"James, we need to get back to the ship," Katherine spoke in my ear. "What if—"

"My lady is right. I need to get back to my crew. Is there anything I can do to be of help to Princess Tiger Lily?"

"Stay out of the Viridianwood." It was an order, not a request. "The guard won't hesitate to cut you down."

"Last time I checked, I was a free man. I'll do as I please." I made to leave, keeping myself between Kat and Dain.

"Jas," I turned to look back at him. "I'll be sure to tell Peter you're here."

"No!" I responded a bit too quickly. "I...I want to keep it a surprise. It's been ages since we've seen each other."

"Have it your way." Dain grinned. "Stay out of trouble, Jas," he warned and sauntered off back toward the village.

I breathed out a sigh of relief the moment he was gone. The last thing I wanted was for Peter to know my whereabouts.

A rogue band of Lost Boys? Peter clearly hadn't changed his ways. His own Lost Boys were going rogue? At least that meant more of them were surviving. Either the Lost Boys were getting smarter, or Peter was losing his edge. That explained why the camp was so quiet. They, too, must have been out looking for them. Ironically, if I had just appeased Kat, I might have found exactly what I was looking for.

"Why did you ask that man not to tell Peter you are here?"

"Dain is no man," I chuckled. "He is fae, like most of the beings here. I asked him not to tell Pan so I could have the advantage of surprise. However, he is a sentry for the Princess. I can assume he'll report my arrival to Tiger Lily. Her loyalties are with Peter—"

"So, he'll likely tell Tiger Lily, and she'll tell Peter."

"Exactly. We need to get back to the *Jolly Roger* and devise a plan."

CHAPTER FIVE
-STRANGERS-
James

~

D awn had just barely begun to peek through the window, casting our cabin in shades of grey. It was a welcome sight. I had been awake, lying in bed for hours. Katherine was tucked into my side. A spray of her hair tickled my chest, but I made no move to disturb her. My return to Neverland had rattled something within me. Reopened an old wound that had never healed. Now, it festered, and I was anxious. After a fitful night, I still hadn't devised a solid plan to achieve what I wanted.

I'd been back for one day, and I had yet to lay eyes on

Pan. I reminded myself that I'd waited years for my revenge. It was useless to rush through it now. I wanted to savor it. Let it consume me until it filled all the cracks in my soul. Only then would I be whole.

Kat stirred beside me. A soft coo fell from her lips as she woke.

"Did you sleep well, my beautiful girl?"

"Never better," she sighed, tracing her fingers over my chest. No hint of the irritation she'd had last night when I'd acquired the pixie. Apparently, all sins were forgiven. Her patterned circles moved lower with each caress. I grabbed her dainty wrist, halting her downward progress.

"You keep that up, and I'll tether you to this bed and worship you for the rest of the day."

She pulled away from me, sitting up. The pouty look on her face was utterly adorable. "What makes you think that's not exactly what I was going for?"

The morning light pooled around her wild mane of blonde hair. In a flash, I grabbed her, flipping her down on the bed. The sound of her startled yelp had my heart pounding faster. My fingers dug into her arms, pushing her into the mattress. I positioned myself between her legs just so my hard cock pressed against her softness. She moaned and arched her back into me.

"You little minx," I chided as I bit her neck. "You'll be the death of me, woman."

"I will enjoy every minute of claiming your soul."

"Mmm," I grumbled as I rolled off her, reluctantly

breaking her spell on me. "We have a mission today, remember? We cannot let the lead on these rogue Lost Boys go cold."

"Are you sure, James? We have all the time in the world to get back at Pan."

"No, it must be today."

"Why do I get the feeling that all the skeletons in your graveyard have awoken from the dead?"

I huffed at her appraisal. She was spot on, but I wasn't about to admit it. At least not to her.

"Tell me what's eating at you. I could help you. Let me make an incantation to banish all your negative energy. I'll even dance around naked to bind it." She arched a brow at me, trying to lighten my mood. When I remained silent, she reached to tuck a lock of my hair behind my ear, but I flinched away from her. I didn't want her to see the full depth of the darkness living inside me. Once I settled everything with Pan, then I could heal and become the man she deserved.

I got up from the bed, pretending to ignore the hurt look in her eyes while I slid on my pants and strapped on my cutlass. "I'll be back as soon as I can."

"No. I'm coming with you. You need me," she insisted. I closed my eyes and let out a deep sigh. She would slow me down and it would put her in unnecessary danger, but she was right. I needed her abilities in case this band of Lost Boys wasn't cooperative.

"Get yourself dressed. Something suited to travel." As I

spoke, she was already bouncing out of bed. A smile plastered on her face as she put on one of my linen shirts. She hobbled around the room in an attempt to pull on a pair of tight-fitting breeches she'd found in the storeroom. I cocked a half smile, thoroughly amused at her enthusiasm.

"I just need to pull my hair back, and I'll be ready, *Captain.*"

I rolled my eyes at the exaggerated use of my title. "Meet me topside in ten. I won't wait a moment longer."

"ARE you sure this is entirely necessary, Captain?" Starkey asked. "There's something about these woods. They're pure evil. I'd wager my life on it."

We stood at the edge of the Viridianwood. I, too, felt the dark magic radiating from the forest. The ill feeling nestled into my gut, and I swallowed hard to keep my breakfast down. But it couldn't be helped. I needed to know what Peter Pan had been up to since I'd been gone. If I could get my hands on these truly lost boys, they would be a wealth of information. Another step closer to hitting Pan where it really hurt. Besides, Kat and I had made a promise to give these forgotten boys a safe haven. I would stake my claim on the island and take Pan down with his own men by my side. It was rather poetic, really.

I shot a sideways glance at Starkey. "Did the afterlife make you soft?"

"I just got back. I'm not ready to return so soon, is all," he said as he shouldered past me, taking the lead.

"Stay close behind me, Katherine. These woods are—"

"The embodiment of darkness," she finished for me. "Please tell me we won't be staying long."

"As long as it takes. But you don't have to worry. I know these woods like the back of my hand."

We pushed deep into the heart of the forest, where the thick canopy blocked out the sun, casting its crooks and crevices into deep shadows. I had been away from Neverland for too long. My footfalls were too loud. Each poorly placed step had branches cracking under my feet. A beacon for the nefarious magic that lived here. Aside from Blackbeard himself, there was very little that I had been afraid of. Now, the cautionary tales the fae had told about the Viridianwood began to haunt me. It wasn't the rough terrain that had my heart racing.

"This forest has eyes," Kat said, her gaze scanning in every direction. "And why are there so many bones littered about?"

"They say an old hag calls the forest home. A witch." I raised my brow at the word. Katherine, herself, had been branded a witch. Even though she was something more than human, she wasn't fond of the label.

I stooped down and picked up a segment of jawbone from some unlucky animal. Turning it over in my fingers, I noted the molars were still intact.

"Story has it, she's a bone collector. She gets her power from them. Many young fae have been lured into these woods over the years, never to return again. The natives used to bring offerings and leave them at the edge of the forest to appease her. Apparently, they still do. That's why there are so many," I reassured her. Hoping that the alarm crawling up my spine didn't make its way into my voice.

"And you think that a pack of outcast Lost Boys would choose to seek shelter here? Seems like they are trading one inevitable death for another," Katherine countered as she turned to look at me. Her eyes widened in shocked horror a moment before the sharp edge of a blade bit into my neck.

"If you know these woods don't take kindly to strangers," a deep voice growled in my ear, "then you best be explainin' what you're doing here?" he demanded, a faint Irish lilt to his speech. A clear declaration that this was indeed a man from my own realm and not fae.

The cool metal of his blade against my throat was a welcomed relief in the heat of the forest. The act of aggression ignited the demon within, and the rush made me feel alive. With Pan just out of my grasp, I was eager for a chance to let off some steam.

"Don't make me ask again?" The stranger grumbled, tightening his grip on my shirt.

Mason, Cecco, and Starkey encircled Katherine, blades drawn and eyes alert, while Kat's eyes fixated on me. Wide and blown out with fear, like a fawn in the jaws of its prey. I found myself distracted by how pretty that fear looked on her face, and it made my cock twitch in my pants. An obscene time to be thinking of such things, but I couldn't deny that the thrill of it all was stimulating.

I should have reassured her that everything was fine. A single man posed little threat to us, but I enjoyed that look on her face too much. Not to mention that my return to Neverland had been less than satisfying, and now I had the chance to have some fun.

"Come now, is that really how you greet strangers? Have a little more tact," I quipped, a half-cocked smile pulling at my lips. "At least give me the decency of facing me like a man."

"I regret to inform you, but I lost my decency long ago." The man whistled in my ear, and four more emerged from the shadows. Now, the odds shifted to their favor, but by the looks of the ragtag bunch, we'd make quick work of them if they pressed their luck. They were young, barely more than teenagers, if that. They had to be the Lost Boys that aged out of Peter's ridiculous gang. These were the lucky ones.

"Ah, then we are one and the same. And by the looks of it, I would venture to say we have a few things in common."

"You're testing my patience. Last chance before I run you through," the man seethed, his hot breath thick against my cheek.

"Just finish him off. We can't take any chances," one boy called.

"Hold your tongue, Brix," he barked before turning back

to me. "Who are you, and what are you doing in the Viridianwood?"

"If you'll allow me just one more word—Pan."

"What about him?"

"He owes me a life."

His blade hesitated at my throat for a heartbeat until he finally relented, releasing his hold on me. Before I could whirl on my would-be attacker, his boot planted solidly on my back. With a quick shove, I was on my knees. The hoots and hollers of his men echoed off the trees.

I'd made a vow never to kneel before another man. I'd die before I broke that promise. I was on my feet in a flash, and before the man even registered the threat, my fist connected to his bearded jaw. The blow sent the hulking man down on one knee. "Are we done now?" I asked, pulling my dagger in one fluid motion, prepared for his counterattack. "I'm not your enemy, old man."

"Don't just sit there. Take him out!" The one they called Brix shouted, but the man remained on his knee.

He ignored the cocky little fucker, inspecting his jaw and dabbing at the blood leaking into his thick beard, turning the strands of gray to red. I wasn't sure what to expect, but it definitely wasn't the hearty chuckle that rolled from his lips.

That wasn't the only thing that struck me as odd about the man. He was too old to be a Lost Boy. From the looks of him, I'd say middle-aged. His dark hair, peppered with gray, was slicked back into a ponytail. The sides were clean-shaven, reminding me of a savage Viking. The sun bronzed his weathered skin, and lines of a desperate life were etched across his face. He adjusted a pair of cloudy spectacles, pushing them up his nose as he took measure of my character.

"I still don't believe you've graced me with your name yet, stranger?"

"The name's James. And might I have the pleasure of *your* name, sir?"

"Alfred Acton Smee," he stated gruffly as he got to his feet and offered me his hand. "The boys call me Smee." My eyes flicked to the unkempt bunch. They appeared even more juvenile as they fidgeted. All but the little pissant, Brix, who glared at me and did nothing to hide the scowl on his face.

To settle the tension, I obliged and shook Smee's hand. The possibility of a new alliance took shape with his firm handshake.

"I believe a man such as yourself can understand the need to be overly cautious," he explained, all the while keeping my hand in his crushing grip. "At ease, boys. Let's give Mr. James a chance to explain. This is Jukes, Cookson, Mullins, and Brix," he said as he pointed to the boys. "I ain't never seen you on the island before, and it's a small island. What's this life you say Pan owes you?"

"You're a fool, old man. He's probably in league with Pan, and you welcomed him right in. About all he's good for is that hot piece of ass he brought with him," Brix ranted.

I cocked my head as I appraised the boy. My sanity was hanging on by a thread. I stalked over to him, calculating how many painful ways I could end his life. With his shirt clutched in my fist, I lifted him off the ground until we were face to face.

"Now, now, the boy didn't mean nothing by it," Smee said as he took a step toward us, trying to regain a grasp on the situation. The muscle in my jaw ticked. I had a short fuse when it came to Katherine. But I needed information. If I killed this boy now, I'd never be able to forge a deal with the rest of them.

"This is the only warning you get. Do not look at her. Do not talk about her. Don't even think about touching her. If you cross me, I'll take pleasure in stripping your skin from your body. Do you understand me?"

He nodded quickly, and I set him back on the ground before shoving him backward.

Smee moved in, grabbing the grubby boy and backhanding him like a petulant child. "Apologize to the lady right now and keep your fecking gob shut. Or you'll wish Pan had taken you out when he was done with you."

The shock and humiliation on his flushed face drew a sinister smirk to my lips.

"Sorry, milady," he grumbled, his eyes never leaving Smee's. Insincerity rang clearly in his voice.

Smee turned to me. He had the decency to look ashamed for the actions of his man. "My apologies to you as well, Mr. James. Some are still learning how to behave outside of Pan's fantasy world. Now, you were about to tell me what business you have with Pan. I am interested in hearing what you have to say."

"Not sure there's time for the full story, but let me be clear, no one hates Peter Pan more than I. I may have been lost to Neverland for a time. But I've returned to seek my revenge."

The man eyed me warily before the tense set of his shoulders eased. Pan had wronged this man in one way or another. I could see it in his eyes. It was all the leverage I needed to form a useful alliance. But if these *were* Pan's rejects, they wouldn't have aged significantly since I'd left Neverland's shores. I had been the first Lost Boy. This man was older than me, and he hadn't been in Neverland when I left. His presence here was a mystery.

"Welcome back to the island, Mr. James. Would you and your entourage care to join us for a bit of mead at our camp? We may be of use to each other?"

"The enemy of my enemy is my friend. As you said, this is a small island, and I could use as many allies as I can find. Lead the way."

CHAPTER SIX
—FEALTY—
James

T he camp, if you could even call it that, was situated in a glade of ancient oaks. There was nothing more than a few thatched lean-tos camouflaged with foliage around a central fire pit. The wayward boys had shown us their best attempt at hospitality. A few meager rations rounded out their idea of a feast. It gave a new meaning to the idea of living rough, and I wondered how long they'd called this place home.

Smee situated himself on a stump while the others settled in for the night. They obviously hadn't entertained any guests since they'd been relegated to the forest. They looked starved for news of the outside world. And the idea of a group of strangers with a vendetta against Pan was a truly exciting story. There hadn't been a private moment to speak to my men, but a few pointed looks were all they needed to keep up their guard. I would wager these boys had all been enamored with Pan at one time. Even I hadn't seen past his charm. And I wouldn't be truly at ease until I determined if any of that loyalty remained.

I kept Katherine close to my side. The warmth of the evening had left her skin dewy, and the way my white linen shirt clung to her body drew more than a few interested glances from the young men. Not to mention the comments from that bastard, Brix. She was temptation wrapped in a beautiful package. One I'd succumbed to myself. I may have been a fucking hypocrite, but I'd be damned if I let any of them touch what's mine.

The other boys hadn't so much as spoken a word to me since we reached camp. A husky fellow covered in tattoos approached me. Wary eyes peered out from under a mop of dark curls as he handed me a clay jug. Aside from Smee, he was the oldest of the younger men, and I found myself instantly curious. What stories did these boys have to tell? Were they similar to my own?

Nothing had changed. Pan was still the only player in his sick and twisted game. The one rule still held firm over his band of boys—never, ever grow up.

"It's only mead," he said when I was too slow to bring the drink to my lips.

His words pulled me from my thoughts, and I brought the bottle to my nose. The tang of alcohol and honey wafted up. "One can never be too sure," I countered. "You're Jukes, right?"

"Yes, sir," he mumbled.

"Made that mead myself," Smee announced, cutting off Jukes. It was all he needed to fade back into the shadows of the firelight.

I took a hearty pull from the jug. The harsh liquid warmed my gut instantly. That would be the only time I indulged tonight. I needed my wits about me.

"I appreciate the hospitality, Smee. But to be honest, I am here for more than pleasantries and polite conversation," I said quickly. I needed answers before I showed my cards. "Tell me, how is it that a mortal *man finds* himself in Neverland without the aid of Peter Pan?"

"And what makes you think he didn't help?"

"Peter has no interest in grown men."

"I wasn't always this way. I've been on the island a long time."

"Do you take me for a simple man, Smee?" I asked as I pulled my knife from my belt and began cleaning my nails. "Might I remind you that allies don't lie to one another, and I expect you need this alliance more desperately than I do. Maybe you'd like to try again?"

Tension spread over the group, thick and suffocating.

Their eyes flicked around the campfire, lingering mostly on Cecco, who looked strangely feral in the firelight.

Smee grunted, "You're an intriguing man, Mr. James. Why do I get the feeling that you're more entrenched in this than even I can fathom?"

"Then I'd say you're more astute than I gave you credit for. Give me your story, and if I find you to be valuable, I'll give you mine."

"He took my son."

His words brought me up short. That was a scenario I'd never considered. I masked my shock as quickly as it graced my face.

"Your son?"

"Aye. My boy was only eleven when Pan darkened our window and stole him from me."

"How did you manage to find your way across the veil?" I asked, smothering the swell of jealousy that tried to bubble up from my dark soul. This seemingly ordinary man found a way to Neverland in a much shorter order than I had.

"Sold my soul to the devil. Well, at least he may as well have been. At the time, I was naïve to the worlds beyond our own. But stories of the fae run deep in the borough. I tracked one down and wagered a price for my passage across the veil."

"And your son, where is he now?"

Smee held my gaze, his jaw working as he wrangled the emotion that showed clearly on his face. "I ain't found him as of yet."

"All these years you've been on the island, and you still haven't found him. Are you sure he's even still here?"

Smee broke my stare. His jaw worked as he digested my words. I hadn't meant to be harsh, but I was in no mood to entertain sob stories. "If your son isn't on the island, why haven't you returned home?" I pressed.

"Home to what? My son *was* my home. Without him, I have nothing. Besides, when I arrived, I realized it was more than just my son who needed help. And I've been doing my best to save these boys from the same fate as…" He couldn't finish the sentence. Couldn't admit openly that his son was likely long dead. "Maybe I was waiting for you? Because I believe you're about to change all that for me."

The rest of the evening was full of stories that poured out of them just as freely as the mead. Each one with a slightly different version from the previous, but they all ended the same. Neverland had begun to rob the older boys of their memories, but they still retained enough to paint a clear picture. Peter had been busy, and the sheer number of boys he discarded over the years had my demon flexing in my chest.

I listened in rapt interest to every word they said. The alcohol freed their minds and loosened their tongues. While I made mental notes of their stories, my old memories began to resurface. I wondered idly how long it would take for Neverland to dull them, which only ignited my sense of urgency. If I was doomed to forget my past, I needed to be sure I killed Pan with a clear conscience. While my hatred for him remained intact.

"I am knackered," Smee yawned. "About time to get some shuteye, boys. We'll continue this in the morning. Mr. James," he bade me goodnight and ambled off into a darkened corner of the camp.

It was late, but my mind was racing. And there was no way I'd let my guard down here. Katherine had long since fallen asleep. I'd tucked her into one of the lean-tos and excused myself. Finding a dark spot just far enough to keep an eye on Kat but not disturb her with my fidgeting.

I was lost in thought as the night shifted into the early morning hours. That's when the shadows caught my attention. I almost ignored it. The fire had been casting eerie shadows over the camp all night. I rubbed my tired eyes, but this was no trick of light. A shadow was coming for my girl. I watched carefully, clutching my dagger so tightly the hilt dug painfully into my palm. I moved silently, cloaked in darkness, until I was close enough that the dying embers of the fire illuminated the threat.

I stopped in my tracks. Apparently, my warnings had fallen on deaf ears. That little fucker, Brix, was kneeling by Kat, pulling her blanket down with one hand while the other was moving obscenely inside his pants.

My vision turned red, and my self-control evaporated into the ether. I pulled a cigar from my pouch, and before he could lay his filthy hands on my girl, I struck a match. The scrape and splutter of the fire sounded unusually loud in the quiet of the camp. Brix jumped at the sound, his eyes going wide as the flame illuminated my face in the darkness.

"You've been quite a naughty boy, haven't you, Brix?" I drolled, my voice deadly calm.

"I—I can explain," he stammered.

"James?" Katherine sat up; her voice clouded with sleep as she tried to figure out what was happening.

"Nothing to worry about, love. Apparently, Pan never taught him any manners. Did he, Brix? He never told you not to put your hands on things that don't belong to you? That's precisely why you needed a mother." I pulled a deep drag off the cigar, the cherry red ember flaring in the darkness.

"You don't know what you're talking about. You didn't see a thing."

"What's the story here?" Smee's deep voice cut in.

As much as I respected the man, I'd sworn to protect Katherine. That, mixed with my own jealous rage, had already decided the boy's fate. The commotion had awakened the entire camp, and they gathered to watch the spectacle.

"Brix here wagered that I wasn't a man of my word. What's worse, he thought so low of me that he didn't expect I would always be ready to protect what's mine."

"No, it wasn't like that. I never touched her!"

"What do you think, Katherine?" I started as I stalked toward my prey. "Should I skin him alive or sacrifice him to the bone faerie? I'll let you choose."

"James, I don't think this—"

"Peter taught me to take what I wanted," Brix interrupted. "No reason a girl like her should be stuck with an old man when she can have a Lost Boy like me."

"So, you admit it, you're still a Lost Boy? Because if you think Pan will ever take you back, you truly are lost."

"He *will* take me back. Once a Lost Boy, always a Lost Boy," he said pridefully before letting out a raucous crow.

I shook my head, a chuckle coming out of me at his naïvety. "Crow all you want. He won't be coming for you." Brix would always be an immature boy at heart. And that heart belonged to Pan. "You're a sorry excuse for a man. Still pandering to a boy who would prefer you were dead. The only thing you've learned is to treat people as though they're nothing more than toys to be played with. But you can give your apologies to the Divine when you meet them."

"You're no better! Even as a boy, Peter Pan is more of a man than you'll ever be!" he seethed.

Something inside me snapped, and the young man before me transformed into Peter. A lifetime of tragic memories breached the floodgates of my mind, drowning me in their darkness. His auburn hair was a mess around his head, falling into mischievous umber eyes that taunted me. But it was his cocky smile that broke my fragile hold on reality. Before I could contemplate my actions, my dagger was in motion. I slit his throat in one swift flick of my wrist. A sneer pulled at my lips as his cocky smile fell away.

The hot splatter of blood across my face pulled me from my downward spiral. Brix slumped to his knees, a river of crimson ruining his shirt. His last gurgled breaths filled the silence of the forest.

My gaze instantly turned to Kat. Her eyes were wide, and the color had drained from her cheeks. I could just make out the tremble in her lip, the quiver betraying her struggle to maintain composure. Was I no better than Peter fucking Pan? Had I proven that to her at this very moment? She thought I was a monster. I could see that clearly. But I was only a monster of Pan's making. And the only way to tame the beast within me was to kill its maker.

"Let me make myself very clear," I started, breaking the hushed silence that settled over the group. I stooped low enough to clean my blade off on Brix's sleeve, driving home the threat without a single word. "Peter Pan, and anyone who follows him, is as good as dead. I will cleanse the island of that infernal boy and wipe his memory from Neverland's history.

If you want to join me, pledge fealty to me as your captain. I can offer you a home on my ship, the Jolly Roger. Ensuring your safety, security, and full bellies. I will give you the sense of family that Pan robbed from you. Not to mention the chance to get the vengeance you so justly deserve."

The men shifted on their feet. Their eyes darted to one another and, ultimately, to Brix's lifeless body before Jukes finally spoke up.

"Does that mean I get to kill Lost Boys, too?"

I nodded solemnly. The idea of killing young boys wasn't

something that sat well with me, but I wouldn't let anything, or anyone, get in my way. And if the Lost Boys were a casualty of war, then so be it.

"I'm in," Jukes said, clamping a hand over his heart.

"Me too!" Mullins chimed in.

"And me," Cookson added.

"Smee?" I asked. The older man had kept silent, allowing the group to make their own decisions. I'd just slaughtered one of the boys he'd worked so hard to save. I couldn't be sure I hadn't ruined any chance of an alliance between us. "I can't make any promises. But if you follow me, I will find you answers about your son."

"Honored to be at your service, Captain."

CHAPTER SEVEN
-POISON-

Katherine

etween his obsession with Pan and the addition of four new crewmen, James had his hands full. I'd been given the menial task of keeping our caged pixie cared for. It was likely to keep me quiet on the subject. At least this way, I could ensure she would be treated with kindness and respect. I was still struggling with the idea of her being kept like a pet, but James insisted, and I didn't want another reason to argue with him.

She was a pretty little thing. Pointed ears poked out from her dark brown hair. Chocolate-colored freckles dotted her olive-toned cheeks, drawing attention to the specks of brown in her hauntingly grey eyes. Her delicate wings reminded me of a dragonfly, translucent and glass-like, reflecting the most beautiful iridescent shades of peacock green and blue. She was magic incarnate. I could admire her for hours. But despite her luminescent appearance, she was shrouded in melancholy. She sat silently on the floor of her cage with her knees pulled to her chest.

"Oh, little pixie, please don't be sad. I'll do everything I can to keep you comfortable," I said, hoping she understood my words. I had no idea how to effectively communicate with her. "I wish I knew your name."

Her head hung low as faint tinkling bells surrounded her.

"My heart breaks for you. I was caged once, too." I knew exactly how she felt. Too many times in my life, I'd been held against my will. And here I was, ensuring this poor creature had the same fate.

She stood up, gripping the bars, staring at me with disbelief. Tinkling bells filled the air once again.

"I don't understand." I shook my head.

She sighed and sat back on the floor, clearly frustrated with my lack of comprehension.

"I'm sorry. I'm not from this realm."

She looked at me curiously. Then promptly threw herself back on the floor dramatically in a poof of glittering dust.

There had to be a better way. "I have an idea. If you're willing to try."

She sighed in apparent frustration.

"If you'll let me touch you."

She turned her head to look at me. Her interest clearly piqued.

"I can—see things." She was going to think I was mad. But maybe I truly was mad. I was the one carrying on a conversation with a pixie, who James had likened to a lowly firefly. "If I can touch your hand, I might be able to learn some things about you. It's worth a try."

She smiled and offered her tiny hand to me without getting up. Reaching in through the bars, I placed a finger in her tiny palm. Grief washed over me.

A field of bones.

A tiny, winged skeleton.

Chaos.

James' lifeless body.

A glistening pool of aubergine.

I yanked my hand from the cage, shaking off the unsettling image of James. Something horrific was in the cards for him. I paused to take it all in and gather my thoughts. Reminding myself that my visions were often cryptic and didn't necessarily show mirrored reflections of the future. Later tonight, I'll sketch what I'd seen. If James was being honest and Neverland was going to steal my memories, I wanted documentation to refer back to. I took a settling breath and focused on the little pixie.

Tinkling bells quickly morphed into familiar words. "My name is Meadow."

My eyes widened as I realized I could understand her

clearly. Connecting to her through a vision must have opened up the channels in my mind. "Your name is Meadow? I'm Katherine."

"Oh, now you can understand me?" she asked flippantly.

"Yes!" I giggled. "I didn't know that was going to happen."

She gave a condescending chuckle. "Thank the Divine it did. I'm no good at charades." She stood up, smoothing out her leafy green dress. "Yes, my name is Meadow."

"Pleasure to meet you, Meadow. Are you okay? I felt abundant sadness when I touched you."

"Well, I was better before *he* trapped me in this cage."

"His name is James. I tried to reason with him. I never wanted to—"

"I know it wasn't you. I saw it all over your face the night he captured me."

"I know there is more to your story. I saw…" I wasn't sure how to say it. I was pretty certain she had lost someone important to her.

"You saw, Porthos." Her entire demeanor shifted, and the melancholy shroud returned. "He was my one true love. He didn't deserve to die. Not like that." She drifted off into thought, and a single tear slid down her face. "I was mourning him when…"

"When James captured you," I finished for her.

"Yes."

"Meadow, I'm so sorry. Would you like to talk about it? About Porthos?" I genuinely wanted to help. I couldn't imagine the pain she was feeling, losing her mate.

"Can you bring him back?" she asked with hope in her eyes.

I slowly shook my head. "I cannot. I don't possess that kind of power." My heart broke for her. If I'd lost James, I would die trying to bring him back from the grave.

"What good is talking about it then?" Meadow sighed. She was right. There was nothing I could say that would ease her pain. "Could you possibly bring me outside? I'm fae. I belong in nature. Maybe I'll feel his presence out by the trees."

"That I can do. I was planning to collect a few herbs anyway." I'd been considering concocting a poison to help James finish Pan once and for all. If I could get his attention back to me, we could finally start our happily ever after. I was quickly growing tired of feeling like a second thought. "Maybe *you could* help me find what I'm looking for?"

"Yes! I can show you where to look. Let me out of this cage, and we'll fly to the forest together."

"I'm afraid you'll have to stay in the cage. I don't possess the key."

Her luminescence dimmed at my words. I was all too familiar with that kind of disappointment.

"Besides, I don't know how to fly," I admitted sheepishly. James had promised to teach me once we got to Neverland, but we hadn't had the time. He hadn't had time for much of anything since we arrived. Anything other than finding Pan.

"Flying is easy."

"Says the winged pixie," I teased.

"With my dust and a happy thought, it will be easy for you, too." Meadow suspended herself in mid-air and spun around like a pirouetting dancer. A cascade of sparkling dust fell to the bottom of her cage. "Scoop some up."

"Wait, we're doing this now?"

"No better time than now. I long for the outdoors. Come on, rub some dust on your cheek."

"Umm…" I considered her words for a moment before I decided she was right. James was off somewhere hunting for Peter. I had no logical reason not to. "Okay, let's do it." I smeared the dust across my cheek and waited for further instruction.

"Now, all you have to do is think a happy thought."

I closed my eyes and envisioned my future with James. Just us, no more obstacles, no more distractions.

"That's it! See, I told you, flying is easy."

I opened my eyes to find myself floating effortlessly above the floor. My limbs felt completely weightless, and butterflies were fluttering in my belly. "Meadow! I'm flying!" A giggle spilled from my lips as I glided around the room, getting a feel for being off the ground. It was a truly magical experience. Tucking my knees to my chest, my body tumbled into a mid-air somersault. "I can't believe I'm actually flying."

"You're a natural. It usually takes days to master a flip! Now, grab my cage, and we'll head into the woods. You should practice without the confines of the room. It's much more fun without walls to hold you back."

MEADOW, like James, had refused to take me into the Viridianwood. "The Viridianwood is home to the darkest fae," she had said. "If I take you out there and something happens to you, I'll meet a fate far worse than living in this cage." It was true. If something happened to me, James would blame Meadow. I didn't want to imagine the horrors he could instill upon her.

She had taken me back to the Mysterious River, promising me a varied collection of useful flora within a few feet of the riverbank. Datura, Belladonna, Lily of the Valley, and my personal favorite, Rosary Pea. All species I was pleasantly surprised to find here in Neverland. All lethal and abundantly available. I even collected a few I'd never heard of at Meadow's recommendation.

"These are all highly poisonous choices. What are you planning to use them for?"

I froze. I wasn't expecting our little pixie to be so observant. I didn't want her privy to our desires. I had to think quickly. "Just rebuilding my resources. I like a healthy apothecary at my disposal. You never know what one might need. Besides, not all poisons are bad."

She paused for a moment. "Can we do this again? I'll show you everything Neverland has to offer."

I stifled a sigh of relief that she hadn't tried to pry any further. "I'd like that. I could use some help learning the local flora." Befriending Meadow was proving to be a valuable commodity. I'd just have to keep her in the dark until James' obsession was satiated. "Do you know Peter Pan?" I asked, hoping to gain some insight on our nemesis.

"Of course, I know Peter Pan," she huffed, seemingly offended that I'd ask such a question. "Don't you?"

"I'm hoping to meet him soon. James is an old friend of his. Unfortunately, we haven't been able to find him. Would you happen to know where he is?"

Meadow blew a breath through her nose. "Peter is often off on an adventure by himself. Sometimes, you can find a trail of dead bodies in his wake." She spoke the words nonchalantly, as though leaving a trail of dead bodies was a completely normal thing to do.

"Dead bodies?"

"He does it all the time."

"So, he just goes around killing people?" What kind of monster was he?

"People, beasts, fae, he's not particular," she said casually. "If you're in his way, and *he* is—in a mood." She dragged her thumb slowly across her neck and made a slicing sound before dramatically falling to the floor with her tongue lolling out the side of her mouth. I couldn't help but giggle at her dramatic antics.

A loud crowing off in the distance pulled us from our conversation. Meadow jumped up from the floor, a smile across her face. "That's our Pan now."

"What?" My stomach dropped, and my pulse began to race.

"That crowing is Pan," she confirmed.

Panic consumed me. I couldn't meet him here, not without James' protection. "We should go. Now." I reached into the cage and swiped up more faerie dust, quickly smearing it across my cheeks.

Happy thoughts, think happy thoughts.

"Katherine?" Meadow looked at me, confused. "Is everything okay?"

"It's... I'm... We need to get back. I don't want James to worry. No one knows where I am."

I had stupidly left the Jolly Roger without telling a soul. I didn't even leave a note. What was I thinking? If James returned and I was missing, he would likely fear the worst. I remembered the vision of James screaming in agony. I had made a mistake leaving without notice. And with a stranger, no less. What if this was a trap? I had to get back to the ship. I took a deep breath, closed my eyes, and shifted my thoughts to happier times.

I ANXIOUSLY PACED our cabin while the vision of James lifeless haunted my thoughts. Candlelight flickering off the heavy drapes and dark wood gave an eerie feeling to the room, adding to my unease. It had been a while since I last read him. I should try again and see if things have shifted. Maybe the Divine was ready to reveal more of his story.

"We were close today, Kat." James bounded in, pulling me close for a quick kiss and instantly soothing my nerves. "We heard his ridiculous crowing. He has to be here." His eyes grew wild with excitement. "I dreamt of his death last night. Now I know exactly how I'll execute the bastard. Do you know what lingchi is?" he asked.

"I don't think I've ever heard the term."

"Death by a thousand cuts." He smiled wickedly. "First, we'll bind him to the mainmast. I'll start with slow, shallow cuts. Just enough to make him beg for forgiveness." James pulled his sword and sliced it through the air. "And then, when he is delusional with pain and dripping with blood, my cuts will get a bit deeper. He'll lose his limbs first. Prolonging his inevitable death and turning him into the literal monster that he is. Piece by piece, he'll lose what's left of his humanity until he is nothing more than a glistening mound of raw, red, whimpering meat. It's genius!"

My stomach turned with the vivid description James had laid out. "Forgive me if I'm wrong, but isn't Peter just a boy? That seems harsh, torturing a young child." I wasn't so sure how I felt about mutilating a child. Even one as vicious as Peter.

His lip curled back, and his brows drew together. "Harsh!? He is a vile *thing*. He will never grow up. Peter has lived more lives than either of us ever will. Hell, he has taken more lives than either of us combined. Don't let his youthful appearance soften you."

"What if I had a better solution? In fact, an easier, quicker option?"

"I don't know how you can do better than lingchi."

"I have procured enough herbs to concoct a lethal poison. A simple meal with the boy, and it's over. You can torture him with words and delight in his panic while the poison takes effect."

James took a seat at the table, poured a glass of rum, and lit his ridiculous cigar contraption without speaking a word. His silence was deafening. In all the years I'd known James, I'd never seen him this venomous. I sat across from him and poured myself a heavy glass.

"Do you not like my idea?" I asked delicately.

"What it lacks in artistic poetry, it makes up for in efficiency." A large plume of smoke billowed out of his lungs. "Why don't you make the poison, and we'll see how I feel once we capture the abomination."

I smiled proudly and finished my glass of rum in one quick toss. We were finally going to put an end to this madness. I sauntered over to James and kneeled in front of his feet. The hollows of his eyes were dark, his brows heavy with worry. I wanted to ease the stress from his mind and bring his attentions back to me. "Let me help you relax. Shift your thoughts to something more pleasurable." I pulled the boots from his tired feet and reached for his breeches. "You're tense. Allow me to—release some pressure."

James sipped his rum silently as he watched me pull his hardness from his pants. "Let me show you how much I missed you today." Staring into his fathomless eyes, I licked my lips before bathing his length with my tongue.

"My cock clearly missed you, too," he groaned as his glistening shaft bobbed in appreciation.

His excitement emboldened me. Having the power to make him weak with need had me writhing with excitement. I teased the tip ever so gently, drawing a gasp from James' lips. Sliding my mouth down his generous length, I took every solid inch of him down the back of my throat.

James growled, gripping the back of my head, and pushed himself deeper. My eyes began to water, and saliva spilled from the corners of my mouth. "Fuck, Kat, I love the way my cock looks in your mouth. So pretty."

His praise melted my core, and wetness pooled between my legs. James continued to guide my head, using me for his pleasure until his breathing became ragged and jerky. I pulled him from my lips, swallowing his salty release, and gasped for a breath.

"How, may I ask, did you procure herbs?"

My heart sank, and a chill ran down my spine. Did he really just dismiss our intimacy and jump right back into Peter? "I'm sorry? Do we need to talk about this now?"

"I'll ask you again, Katherine. How did you procure the herbs?"

I stood up, wiping his cum from my lips. "Can we finish this first?"

"We're finished. Answer my question."

His words stung. I never thought he would dismiss me in a moment of passion. I took a cleansing breath, smoothed out my shift, and prepared for his inevitable reprimanding. He was going to be irate with me for leaving without protection. "I was trying to help," I sighed. "I took Meadow to the river to forage for supplies."

"Meadow?"

"The pixie, her name is Meadow. I read her today, and somehow, I can now understand her tinkling."

"You went exploring? On the island? Alone? Kat, do you have any idea how dangerous that was?"

"I wasn't alone."

"You had a *caged* pixie with you. What if she tricked you? Led you somewhere dangerous?"

"I was simply trying to help. Nothing bad happened. She's actually a lovely companion."

"A companion? She is not a pet. I'll get you a feline if you need a *companion*."

"I found her to be quite helpful. In fact, she's going to teach me about Neverland's local flora."

"I don't like it. Not one bit. If something were to happen to you…" Shaking his head, he stood up and pulled a pistol from a nearby chest. "If you are going to run off on your own, you'll need protection. Do you know how to use a pistol?"

"I know *how to* fire one," I admitted. Blackbeard had taken the time to teach me on *the Queen Anne* on the off chance we were ever in a situation where I might need to. However, I never got the chance to fire it. "Whether or not I can hit something is altogether different. I've never actually pulled a trigger."

"We will practice. I don't want you going off alone without this pistol ever again. Do you understand? If something happens to you, it's on her head. She will suffer my wrath."

"Yes, sir." I had no doubt James would kill Meadow if I were in any way harmed. I'd have to be more careful.

"I've told you before, beautiful things in Neverland are never what they seem. You'd be wise to remember that. Now, let's go to bed. I've got a busy day tomorrow scouting Pan, and thanks to you, I'm relaxed enough to actually sleep."

CHAPTER EIGHT
-GHOSTS-
James

I roused the crew at dawn, unable to contain my excitement a moment longer. Today was the day I found Pan. I could feel it in my bones. We'd started our search along the Mysterious River, trekking into Tiger Lily's territory. I would trade mountainous countryside for rolling seas any day. The prospect of scaling another peak or traversing through another mile of suffocating forest seemed torturous. But my patience had officially run out, and my temper had been on a short fuse. I wouldn't rest until I found Pan.

I'd been on the island for far too long without so much as a glimpse. If Dain hadn't confirmed his presence, I would have been convinced he'd left altogether. He still hadn't returned to his underground home. This I knew for certain. I'd assigned a rotating watch outside the place the moment we arrived. Knowing Peter and his ridiculous games, he could be anywhere. The possibility that he may have crossed the veil in search of new Lost Boys weighed heavy on my mind. Hearing his pathetic crowing yesterday gave me some modicum of comfort. But that comfort was waning with every passing moment.

I was committed to scouring the island until I found him. No stone left unturned. The men fell silent as the hours dragged on, and there was still no sign of Peter or his Lost Boys. Even Katherine had kept up with my staggering pace without a single complaint.

We'd reached the edge of Tiger Lily's lands when frustration drove me to my breaking point. The tenuous grip I had on my temper was quickly slipping. The constant swing of my cutlass had been the only way to forge a path through the dense forest, and my decidedly mortal body was protesting. I gave the signal to stop as I rubbed at the ache radiating across my shoulder. The trees had finally thinned, sweeping into a valley before rising into a daunting mountain range.

I washed my frustration down with a hearty swig from the flask at my belt. The tension eased slightly as the rum warmed my gut. But I was keenly aware of the crew's silence, and it began to eat away at me. They wanted me to give up. They were waiting for me to call off the mission, but I'd be damned if Pan won this victory over me.

"Any chance you're sharing today?" Katherine asked warily as she approached me.

"Share?" I barked. The idea of sharing her with anyone sent an irrational flood of jealousy to my already taxed mind.

"The rum, James. I meant the rum," she said, exasperated.

"Shit, I'm sorry, Kat," I stumbled over my apology as I handed her the flask. "I didn't mean to… I'm just—"

"It's fine. I know Peter's absence is weighing on you. Do you want to talk about it?" She took a swig from the flask, her eyes never leaving mine. I wanted to tell her I was beginning to think I was a failure. I'd spent years of my life planning. I'd traveled between realms for this, and I was losing in the last leg of the race. It was enough to drive me mad.

"There's nothing to talk about. We're on the cusp. I feel it. We'll find him soon." I spoke the lie so eloquently. I couldn't let her faith in me waver. She was starting to doubt me. It was clear. That's why she'd started concocting a poison to finish him off. She was trying to take matters into her own hands. She'd taken measure of me and found me wanting.

"If we don't find him today, there will be another day. Maybe tomorrow we could—"

"Leave it be, Katherine! This isn't any of your concern. I'll deal with Pan on my own. Give me some damn space, woman." The moment the words left my lips, regret welled up inside me. The hurt look on her face tore open my heart. My mind cycled through an assortment of apologies I could offer her when something caught my eye. A flicker of auburn in a sea of green.

"Don't shut me out. I can—"

"Shh." I shoved a finger to her lips, quieting her so I could focus. There it was again. I was sure of it this time. I broke out into a dead run, chasing after my destiny. I heard my men calling after me, but they were merely an afterthought. I had him within my sights, but I wasn't about to let him slip through my fingers.

I barreled back through the forest, flashes of auburn luring me on, but I made no gains on him. My heart pounded in my chest, and my lungs burned, but my legs churned on. While my body toiled, my mind was my enemy. Flashbacks from the last time I thought I had Pan within my grasp at Mag Mel plagued me. Had my mind conjured yet another vision of Peter out of desperation? Was I truly going mad?

Just when I was fully convinced that I was merely chasing ghosts, I skidded to a halt in a clearing. There, crouched on an outcropping of rocks, was Peter Pan.

My breath came in ragged pants as I stared in disbelief. "Pan!"

The boy whirled on me, squinting in the late afternoon sun. The flicker of his pixie circling his head.

"Do I know you?"

I stood there, glaring at the boy who'd been at the center of my world for far too long. My body locked in place as a wave of emotions crashed into me. Rage was something I knew all too well, but there was more to it. A blind sense of nostalgia. An unnatural awareness of being exactly where I belonged in the universe. Most surprising of all was disappointment. It snatched at my throat and stuck there. All these years. All this hate I'd harbored for so long toward the idea of Peter Pan and what he represented, and at the end of it all, was nothing more than a simple boy.

He flitted to the ground from his high perch like a bird, taking a step forward to get a better look at me.

"Careful with this one, Peter." His pixie's words of warning were in sharp contrast to the sweet, melodic sound of bells that flowed like music from her mouth. But he swatted her away dismissively.

"You look familiar. Have I bested you before?" he asked as a cocky smile cut across his face.

"There he is; there's the conceited little bastard I know so well. Even after all these years, your mind is still as infantile as your body."

"Right, so I did best you, and now you're sore about it. Don't think it'll help much, but I'm willing to give you another go at it."

"You really don't remember me, do you?"

"Once I've bested someone, I have no need to remember them. It's a waste of time to look backward."

"And that is why history is doomed to repeat itself."

"History is for old, dusty books. I only care about the next big adventure."

"At the rate you're going, death will be your next big adventure."

"Are you going to talk my ear off or get on with challenging me? I haven't got all day, old man."

"Once upon a time, you promised me a life of fun and adventure," I lamented. He had to remember me, or it would ruin everything. "I was the first boy you lied to."

He scratched his head, trying to remember, but Neverland's magic kept it just out of reach. "Now that I think about it, there have been quite a lot of boys. None of them overly memorable."

I pinched the bridge of my nose. The little fucker was testing my patience. "I know your story from the very beginning. I'm the one who helped you make the rules. You called me—"

"Jas?" The name rolled off his tongue, a quizzical look in his eyes as he took another step closer to me. "Can't be. You're so..." He scrunched his nose and squinted his eyes, really looking at me for the first time. He floated off the ground until we were face to face. His pixie fluttered around us like a possessed house fly, glowing red in her irritation. My hand clutched around the dagger at my belt. I could have ended him at this very moment. But it wasn't time, not yet. He had to know for certain. His soft, brown eyes went wide as recognition finally hit. "Oh, My Divine, how'd you get so old?"

My hand snapped up to grab for him, but he was too quick, pulling back a moment before I had him in my grasp.

"I had the privilege of getting old because I didn't roll over and die when you abandoned me in the gutter," I growled as I drew my cutlass.

"All this time, and you're still sore about it? You're the one who broke the rules."

I pointed my sword at him, inviting him to engage. I was owed a token of revenge, and now the demon within me was ready to collect. "They all break the rules eventually, don't they, Peter?"

"Now that you mention it," he stopped and scratched his head with one hand while he pulled his short sword from his belt with the other, "they've all been terrible at the game. Maybe next time, I shall bring a girl back instead."

"Not a fucking chance!" I swung at him, my cutlass glancing off his sword.

"What happened to your manners, Jas?" Peter tsked as he drifted around me, light as a feather.

"Because of you, I never had a mother to teach me manners."

We moved in a lethal dance, Pan gliding around me effortlessly while I swung my sword in a blind rage. I was one well-placed swing away from ending all of this and devoting my life to Katherine. But the Divine kept him just out of my reach.

"Good form, old man," Pan praised.

"I've had years to practice with this very fight in mind."

"Ahh, but all those years have made you that much slower. Might I interest you in some faerie dust to even the odds?" He offered with a cheeky smirk on his face, and I knew the reason for it.

"I'm not giving him a single grain of dust," the pixie ranted in a tirade of bells.

"Don't worry, Faun. Jas was always the worst at flying. He couldn't do it even if he wanted to." It was a low blow. A sore spot between Pan and I. Instantly, I was a child again with all of my flaws on display. Humiliation eating away at me.

I swallowed hard, but my face remained stoic. I'd learned to hide my emotions so well over my lifetime that it took little effort to slam a mask in place and throw all my energy into my sword. Sweat beaded on my brow, stinging my eyes. I'd never felt my age until this moment. Pan's laugh echoed around the forest, making a mockery of me. My life's sacrifice was nothing more than child's play to him.

"James!" The alarm in her beautiful voice cut into my concentration. I turned reflexively at the sound. Katherine stood at the edge of the forest, her chest heaving and her eyes wide with fear. My men emerged from the shadows right behind her. That single distraction was all it took. I heard the whistle of the blade, and I felt it rustle my hair before the sting set in. Warm blood spilled down my cheek and onto my shirt.

His laugh overshadowed the sound of my groan. The little fucker had no honor in the way he fought. I should have remembered that.

"Why, Jas," he started through fits of laughter, "you've

found a mother after all. It's not done a bit of good. You still have no manners."

"Don't you dare bring her into this," I growled, raising my sword again to reengage him.

"Peter, what have you got there?" a juvenile voice called out.

"Oh, Pan, you found us some pirates! That'll be great fun!" called another as several young boys joined us in the clearing. Wide, expectant eyes peered at us from dirt-caked faces.

"Oh, I like this game!" the boys chimed in with agreement.

"You fools, can't you see he's using you?" I barked at them. Irritation flooded me at the sheer naïveté of the boys. "You'll break his rules even if you don't want to."

"Speaking of rules, I think we should add a new one to the list," Pan piped up, commanding the boy's attention away from me. "Pirates—" he paused for effect, and all of them stared at him in rapt interest, hanging on his every word, "are bad!" he finished, and they whooped in approval. Their calls turned into battle cries as they charged my men, some of them wielding wooden swords.

This wasn't a fair fight. My men were ruthless pirates, but killing young boys still wouldn't sit well with them.

"Enough!" I bellowed, the authoritative tone bringing them up short. "Leave Pan and come with me before it's too late."

"This pirate talks too much. Grown-ups always ruin the

game. Let's go back to hunting beasts. I hear the crocodiles are quite ornery this time of year," Pan said with a deep scowl on his face. I'd struck a nerve. If I could turn his Lost Boys against him, that would spoil all of his fun.

Pan turned his back on me, drifting just out of my reach.

"Turn and fight!" I shouted. I couldn't let him walk away now. But he ignored me completely. His boys followed suit behind him like perfect little soldiers, turning their noses up at my offer. "Turn around and fight me, you coward." I stalked after him as my rage boiled over. This wasn't how it was supposed to go. A lifetime of planning for this very moment, and it was all falling through my fingers. "You owe me!"

"Don't worry, old Jas. The game is just beginning." He cracked a cocky smile at me before he jetted away, and I fell to my knees. My mind was a whirlwind. No single thought could take hold in the chaos. Just a string of whispers that were deafening inside my head.

Failure.

Worthless.

Pathetic.

Defeated.

I was frozen in my own hell, waiting for it to stop. I'd questioned my sanity on more than one occasion, but the hiss of voices in my head confirmed that I'd truly tipped over the edge. The feel of cool fingers on my skin pulled me out of the storm. I flinched, throwing off the offending touch.

Whirling on the world, ready to destroy anything and everything.

"James?" The tremble in that sweet voice sliced through the madness, and I found myself peering into emerald eyes. The world, in all its cruelness, came rushing back. The cutlass in my hand quivered as I held it to Katherine's throat. She swallowed hard but stood her ground, staring down the beast that had taken over.

I hadn't fully regained control over my demon, but I managed to drop the sword. A trickle of blood flowed from the nick on her neck. Marking how close my blade had come to ending the only good thing in my life. I drew a shaky breath into my burning lungs, trying to get a hold of myself.

"Love, are you... are you alright?" she asked hesitantly.

I grabbed her arm and dragged her body against mine. A mew of panic escaped her lips but then melted into a moan as my tongue found her throat, licking the blood from her skin. I sucked at the wound, pulling more of her life source into my mouth, the silver tang of her sating my blood lust.

I pulled away just as quickly, wiping her blood from my lips. "Never better, love. If war games are what he wants, then game on."

CHAPTER NINE
-FORGETTING-

James

I t had been a fortnight since the confrontation with Pan that had gone so tragically wrong. I'd spent the better part of that first week buried in planning and plotting. I had discreetly sent letters out across Neverland looking for allies. I was determined to turn the entire island against Pan. Apparently, it was going to take more than one epic battle to settle a lifetime of revenge. If I had to destroy Peter Pan one piece at a time, then that's what I'd do. The scheming was enough to quell my demon for now, but the voices hadn't stopped. I drowned them out the best I could with rum. It was a daily reminder that my mind was truly broken. Given enough time, I could control them. I *had* to control them.

Katherine sat silently across the table from me as she ate her breakfast. She'd been giving me the space I'd asked for. Demanded was a more appropriate description of how it all went down, and I hadn't been nice about it. She busied her days with that damn pixie, the two of them working on the perfect poison for Pan. Her dedication to its creation was an affront to my ego—she didn't believe I could kill Pan on my own.

I did my best to swallow my pride and ignore it, but I'd been failing miserably. I knew she deserved better from me. The fear of losing her, of letting her down, was driving me to desperation. I couldn't let her find out how deeply disturbed I really was. I'd rather push her away now while I sorted out all my faults than lose her forever. I had a lifetime to make it up to her. Even though she was within an arm's length, it felt like we were fathoms apart.

"Katherine—"

A slight rapping at the door interrupted my feeble attempt at small talk. "Come in!" I barked.

The door creaked open, and Smee poked his head in. "Is now a good time, Captain?"

I looked at Kat, ready to dismiss the man if it looked like she would only talk to me, but her eyes never left the food on her plate. The chasm between us was growing, but I could do nothing about that now.

"Yes, yes," I grumbled, waving him into the cabin. The

man had quickly become indispensable. I'd named him as my bo'sun shortly after he'd arrived on the ship. "What news do you have for me?"

"We received a response from the fae. It seems the young princess, Tiger Lily, wants to meet in person to, umm…" He pulled a piece of parchment from his breast pocket and read from the page. "To further discuss your request to kidnap Lost Boys and deliver them to pirates." This got Kat's attention. Her emerald eyes shot up to mine. A look of reproach set into the lines of her brow.

"That's not how I worded it in my letter to her," I assured Kat. "The youth of Neverland are going to drive me to an early grave," I mumbled to myself as I stabbed my fork into the egg on my plate.

Katherine cleared her throat but said nothing, averting her eyes back to her food.

"Did she specify a time and place for this meeting to occur?"

"It says that she will send a member of her Royal Guard to make arrangements."

"Dammit! The fae have no sense of urgency when they live immortal lives. It could be years before she sends for me."

"And another thing, Captain. The supplies we've been storing on the mainland appear to have been ransacked. The men found this note among the remaining scraps." Smee handed me a piece of parchment with scribbled letters that read *Pirats R bad.*

"Goddamned brats! Mr. Smee, drop the men to half rations until we can get the stores replaced. Be sure to grab a bottle of rum from my stash and pass it around. Hopefully, that will compensate for the missing half."

"Aye, Captain. Shall we be expecting you topside soon?"

"I'll be there presently. You are dismissed, Smee."

My attention reverted to Katherine once we were alone. "And what might you be up to today?" I asked. Our conversations of late had been nothing more than pleasantries, but I couldn't think of any other way to break the tension between us.

"Oh, don't worry about me. I'll be spending my day with Meadow." Her every word was punctuated with irritation.

She doesn't want you.

She knows you're worthless.

She can do better.

The voices whispered hideous things in my mind.

"No, no, no!" I pushed back from the table, upending my chair. Katherine startled at my outburst and stared at me wide-eyed.

I froze in place, the room and my mind returning to silence. I had no words to explain what had just happened. "Never mind," I growled before wiping my breakfast from my lap and stalking out of the room.

CONSCIOUSNESS SEEPED into my drowsy mind the following morning. The bustle of the crew as they busied themselves with the day was altogether too loud. I refused to open my eyes and face whatever consequences I'd suffer after drowning my sorrows with an entire bottle of rum the night before. I was surely going to regret sleeping topside with nothing more than a coiled piece of rope as a pillow.

"Good day, Mr. Starkey." Katherine's sweet voice carried on the breeze, and I rolled myself over with a groan. I wasn't ready to face her yet. "Do you know where I might find Mr. James?" I couldn't hear Starkey's response, but I prayed he kept my night's lodging a secret and directed her to wait for me in our cabin.

The shock of cold water ripped me from my drunken stupor. I spluttered and flailed unceremoniously on the deck. The early morning light seemed excessively bright. Before I could wipe the water from my eyes, firm fingers gripped my ear and pulled.

"Ahhh, what the f—"

"I am done waiting for you to grow up and talk to me like a man!" Katherine scolded as she pulled me to my feet by my ear like a child.

"What in the name of the Divine are you doing, woman?"

"You have been acting like a child, and I'm done ignoring it. Why didn't you come to bed last night?"

My vision finally cleared, leaving a brooding Katherine in my line of sight, her breasts heaving with irritation. My eyes reverted to the empty bottle of rum I'd left rolling on the deck. I hadn't been able to face her after my outburst at breakfast. I still didn't know how I was going to explain myself. Drowning my problems in a bottle of rum seemed like a much better idea than facing them head-on. But the look on her face and the pounding in my temples said otherwise.

"I—I must have passed out topside. I may have indulged a little too much."

"You chose rum over me?"

"Can we take this conversation to our room?" Katherine's outburst had drawn curious onlookers. The last thing I needed was for the crew to have a front-row seat to my tumultuous love life.

I wrapped my hand around her arm and started urging her forward. She tore herself from my grip and stormed toward our cabin. Her heeled boots echoed off the planks as she walked.

She paced the room but remained silent until I closed the door.

"Tell me why?" she asked.

"Why what?"

"Why are you shutting me out?"

"I'm not," I lied. "You knew when we arrived in Neverland that I had an agenda."

"Well, maybe you should change your mind. He's only a boy, after all. We can forget all about him and live a good life. Just the two of us."

"You know I can't do that," I growled. Dropping my vendetta against Pan was where I drew the line.

"Why not? I need to know—why can't you let this go?"

"You know all you need to know. Once it's done, then, and only then, can we move on."

"Then let me in. We're in this together. You could help me finish the poison. I've almost perfected it. We're supposed to be a team. Don't you trust me?"

"Yes, but... I'm not myself right now, Kat. I've sworn to protect you, even if that means protecting you from myself."

"Do you love me, James?"

"How can you ask me that? You know I love you."

"You cannot protect me from love. Where you falter, I am your strength, if you would only let me help you."

"I'm not sure I can be helped, Katherine."

"If you truly believe that, then all is lost, and you'd let me walk out of your life forever."

I turned away from her and walked over to the window, the vast expanse of the sea calming me. She was right. I should let her go. The voices in my head confirmed that she was too good for someone like me.

"I can't," I whispered.

"What was that?" she asked, forcing me to repeat myself.

"I can't let you go," I shouted at her, turning from the window and closing the distance between us. My hand pressed firmly against her neck, pinning her to the paneled wall. "Can't you see I am not the hero in this story? If I was, then I'd walk away, knowing you deserved better. But you've fallen for the villain. A selfish, maniacal villain who left his morals at the gates of hell years ago."

"Then tell me what you want. Is it me? Or revenge? Because I'm not sure if there is room in your heart for both."

Something inside me snapped.

"There is no choosing." The words came out low and measured. A warning emphasized in each word. Without another thought, I took her mouth hard and fast. This wasn't a sweet, loving kiss. I devoured her. My lips crushed hers, my teeth catching her lip and biting down until she yelped, but she didn't pull away. She met my fervor with a passion of her own. Her fingernails raked down my scalp and then fisted painfully in my hair. Our tongues clashed in reckless abandon until my mind was swimming with need. My cock pressed painfully against my breeches. I needed to own her. Prove that she was mine in every way. I gripped the bodice of her dress in my fists, and the sound of ripping fabric filled the cabin.

"We won't be needing this. I want to look at what's mine." I pushed the ruined dress off her shoulders and down to her feet before lifting her up and tossing her petite form over my shoulder.

Her tiny fists pummeled at my back. "James, what are you doing?" she yelled. "We're not done talking."

"Oh, kitten, I think we are." I slapped her ass hard to drive home my point. But she continued to protest, kicking her legs wildly, arousing my demon. I loved it when she fought me.

I tossed her on the bed, her breasts bouncing and her hair in a wild mess around her face. She was stunning.

"Ah, ah, ah," I cautioned as she tried to squirm off the bed. I pulled the dagger at my belt, twirling it between my fingers. "You stay put."

"You cannot fix this by fucking me!"

I ignored her for now, walking to the bedside table and exchanging the knife for a length of rope. If she was going to make this difficult, I was going to savor every minute.

"Give me your hand."

"Why?"

I gave her a cautionary look, and without another word, she offered her wrist. I secured one to the bed, followed by the other. Rage swirled behind her emerald eyes. A finely contained tempest.

"This isn't what I want, James."

"Is that so, love?" I challenged, a smug smile creeping across my lips as I crawled on the bed, stalking toward her. She pressed her thighs together, trying to hide what I already knew. I wrenched her legs apart, and just as I expected, she was ripe with desire. Her pink pussy glistened with the arousal she'd been trying to hide from me.

"You think I don't know what you like? That your darkness doesn't speak to my own? You cannot hide from me, Katherine."

Her lips parted, likely another string of questions that were too difficult to answer. I pressed my finger against her lips, halting whatever she was about to say, and pulled a handkerchief from my breast pocket. She jumped when I mopped up her wetness, coating the scrap of fabric.

"Now, open up." Hesitantly, she opened her mouth, and I stuffed the cloth in. "That's my good girl."

I left her on the bed, taking my time stripping off my coat and shirt while I admired the view. My cock throbbed in my pants at seeing her spread out for me. A heady rush clouded my better judgment, pulling out the darkness within me.

I retrieved my blade from the bedside table, pleased as her eyes followed me around the room. I crawled back to her, positioning myself between her legs. She trembled as I dragged the cool metal down her thigh, turning it to tap the flat edge against her clit.

"We're kindred spirits," I said as I continued to tease her with my knife. "We thrive on the edge of fear. It's a potent aphrodisiac, wouldn't you say?"

I flipped the blade in my hand, gripping it until it cut into my palm, and slowly slipped the hilt inside her tight slit. Her eyes rolled in her head, and a muffled moan escaped around the gag in her mouth. The look on her face with my knife inside her was divine. The blade dug into my skin. Blood filled my palm and dripped onto the sheets. I worked her with the hilt, drawing it in and out until her hips were rising to meet each stroke.

"Not yet, love. I want you on my mouth when you cum."

I pulled the hilt out, and her desperate mews of protest brought a smile to my lips. She needed this just as much as I did. I licked her sweetness from the handle, slow and deliberate. A growl rolled up my throat in response.

Once it was clean, I turned the dagger on her. My blood still coated the blade and stood out in stark contrast to her porcelain skin. I added a bit more pressure this time as I dragged it along her inner thigh. Just enough to draw a well of blood from her skin. It was mesmerizing to watch as her very life source mixed with mine. She held perfectly still, pleasure and pain dancing in her eyes.

I dropped my knife, bowing between her legs, finally getting what I craved. The sweet tang of her filled my mouth, and I knew I'd never get enough. I ran my tongue in languid sweeps along her slit, pulling new moans from behind her gag, and I needed more. I found her center of pleasure and worked it. I was merciless, increasing the pace until she shattered underneath me. Her hips bucked and her legs clamped around my head like a vise, riding my face through her climax.

When she released me from her grip, I couldn't wait any longer. I freed my cock from its constraints, the air feeling cool on my heated skin. I coated my length in her wetness. She writhed under me as I rubbed against her overstimulated clit.

"If you love me, that means you take all of me just as I am, no ultimatums," I said as I slid into her, inch by inch. Her greedy pussy clamping down around me. "You take me so well. You were made for me. We fit perfectly." I ground out as I buried myself to the hilt.

I paused there, fully sheathed, until she began to squirm underneath me. I pulled back and slammed home again. My hand found her throat, pressing her into the bed, applying just enough pressure. A symbolic display. In my own way, I owned her just as surely as she owned me. Tears leaked from the corners of her eyes, but there was nothing but trust that stared back at me, and it was my undoing. I continued to fuck her, losing myself in every stroke. The voices were silent. It was only the two of us in this carnal moment. My balls tightened as my climax crested and broke. My hips jerked as she milked every drop from me.

I rested inside her while my breathing returned to normal. She'd given me back my sanity, at least in this moment, and I was grateful for the silence. But I couldn't stay here forever. I got to my feet and collected a washcloth, wiping the smear of our blood from her thighs, leaving a puckered red scratch behind. I meant to clean her, but I couldn't bear to wipe my essence from her. I wanted her to remember me when she got up and felt it dripping down her leg.

I pulled the saturated gag from her mouth. I wasn't sure what to expect, but she remained silent as I moved to untie her wrists. As soon as I released her right arm, I shifted my attention to her left. A stinging slap across my cheek caught me off guard.

"What was that for?"

"For making me like it when I didn't want to. I am not your property for you to stick your cock into whenever you fancy. You cannot fuck me into submission. That's how Blackbeard treated me, and I know you're better than that. That is why I love you."

"Blackbeard?" I asked. My mind reeled as I processed all she'd said. The name sounded so familiar. I knew it was important, but for the life of me, I couldn't put a face to the name.

"Yes, James. Blackbeard," she said, sounding annoyed. But her eyes softened as she realized the name didn't illicit the response she thought it should. "James, I'm talking about Edward. Edward Teach. Surely you haven't forgotten?"

I racked my brain, and the more I pondered over the name, the more the veil of Neverland's magic hid the truth from me. I pressed against it until recognition slammed into me.

"Oh, Katherine, I am so sorry." The idea of what she was trying to say made me sick to my stomach. I rushed to untie her. "Please forgive me. I never meant to… I would never…" I fumbled over my words as I pulled her into my arms. There were no words to defend my actions. Shame crept from the pit of my stomach, choking off any feeble attempt at an apology. I was mortified. Not only had I given Kat a reason to fear me, but I'd forgotten the man who'd made our lives a living hell for years. Damn Neverland magic. How many of my memories had already slipped through my fingers? Things were already becoming fuzzy. How long before I forgot the reason I needed my revenge against Pan?

I rocked Kat in my arms, smoothing her hair down in the process. "Can you forgive me?"

"Of course, I forgive you. That's what it means to love someone, James."

I grunted at that. "I'm still trying to wrap my mind around the concept of love. I know I've been making a mess of things. But I will try to do better. You deserve better."

"Start by telling me something real. Something deep. Something you've never told anybody else."

I sighed and rearranged us on the bed, trying to delay the inevitable moment of weakness that she wanted from me. It wasn't natural to let myself be raw and naked in front of anyone. That wasn't compatible with survival. But if that's what she needed, I had to try. I tucked her in beside me, pulling the sheets up to cover us. Her head rested on my chest, and my eyes lingered on the rolling waves out the window.

"Have I ever told you why I don't like faerie dust?" I started.

She shook her head but remained silent.

"You see, for faerie dust to work, you must have a happy thought. That's what sparks the magic into action. Most everyone can pull at least one happy thought from somewhere. Your parents, siblings, a beloved dog, something. But as life would have it, by the time I met Peter Pan, I had no truly happy thoughts. I was an orphan. Pan was my first friend, but we'd only just met when we set off for Neverland. My mildly happy thoughts were barely enough to get me off the ground. If it hadn't been for Pan pulling me along, I never would have made it across the veil. And he never let me live that down. He always had a good laugh at my expense because I never got any good at flying. Not like he does. Over the years, I began to loathe the stuff."

"And what about now?" she asked tentatively.

"Now?"

"Do you have any happy thoughts now?"

I pulled her in tighter. "Only because of you."

CHAPTER TEN
-MEMORIES-
James

"Five drops!" Katherine barged into our cabin, holding forth a small vial of yellow fluid. "Five drops is all one needs to cease life."

I grabbed the vial and tilted it in my hands. Watching as the viscous liquid coated the glass walls, leaving behind a chartreuse-colored glow. My stomach clenched at the sight, as if it instinctually knew it was a deadly toxin.

I swallowed my animosity and offered her the praise she deserved. Though her chosen method wasn't exactly appeasing my demon's need for violence, I was proud of her, nonetheless. She was a talented alchemist. I couldn't blame her for wanting to end Peter as quickly as possible. She bore the weight of my obsession almost as much as I did myself.

"Well done, love." I placed a kiss on her cheek and offered her a seat at the table. "Tell me, how does it work?"

"We simply need something to suspend it in." She raised her brow. "Wine, maybe? We could demand parley and offer Peter a drink—as a show of good faith. Once he's taken a sip, he will be rendered frozen. Paralysis will be followed by sheer panic as his lungs cease to inflate. Suffocation will be his demise."

I stroked my beard silently for a moment, contemplating her idea. Watching the boy suffocate would definitely entertain my need for malevolence. "Parley leaves too much at play. He'd never accept the drink. But faerie mead—in the form of a 'gift'—from Tiger Lily, perhaps." I felt a smirk pull across my face. This might actually work. "Peter would never suspect the Princess."

"It's decided!" Katherine snatched the vile back, smiling from ear to ear. "We have council with Tiger Lily today, right?"

"Yes," I nodded, "her Royal Guard. Came quicker than I expected. Apparently, the situation with Pan is more important to her than I realized. We'll be headed to her village later today."

"We can grab a bottle of mead while we're in the village.

Maybe Smee could procure a bottle under the guise of stocking the Jolly Roger? Isn't it wonderful, James? Peter Pan will soon be gone from our lives." She spun around, filled with delight as she bounded back to her apothecary.

Soon couldn't come quick enough.

TIGER LILY'S sentries ushered us into the throne room. White stone walls shrouded in climbing ivy were behind her commanding seat, bringing the outside world in. Though the room was large it felt quite small under her commanding gaze.

The bustling village hadn't changed much since I'd been gone, and neither had the Princess. Her beauty had only deepened over the years. The lines of her face were maturing into a coquettish charm. Ethereal honey-toned eyes perfectly complemented her flawless caramel skin, giving her a haunting appearance. A delicate crown of antlers sat upon her head, contrasting against her dark flowing hair. She carried herself with an undeniable confidence.

Nymphs and satyrs lived unbelievably long lives. Though she appeared to be an adolescent, Tiger Lily, like Peter, was over a hundred years old. She was a Divine Chosen, fated to rule Neverland. And if Tiger Lily had any say about it, Peter would someday rule at her side.

"Jas, old friend," she greeted me warmly as I approached her neatly appointed dais. "Welcome to the sovereign's court. Please have a seat. We have much to discuss." She motioned to several brightly colored cushions laid out before her throne. "Your crew have my blessing to shop the village merchants while we talk."

I bowed before her dais, offering my respect. Noticing the guards tucked into every corner and exit. "I'd prefer to stand. Thank you, Princess."

"As you wish. Time away from the island has changed you." Tiger Lily eyed my physique.

"Time in the thirteenth realm moves faster than Neverland. You know this, Princess." My face heated as her gaze lingered too long.

"You've grown." She smiled. "Aging suits you."

"Thank you, Princess." I was quickly tiring of our little reunion. I wasn't here to exchange pleasantries.

"Tell me, James, why would you choose to leave the island? You are mortal, are you not? Do you not value time?"

"We both know I didn't choose to leave." The words came out in a hiss. I was losing patience with the Princess.

"Peter has clear rules."

"Rules the mere humans he brings back to Neverland cannot abide," I rebuked, causing Tiger Lily to scowl.

"Peter is a Divine Chosen. He is inexplicably connected to the island. What makes you think his actions are not fate's desire?"

"Because he's killing innocent Lost Boys," Kat blurted.

"I'm sorry." The princess paused, glaring at Katherine. "I don't believe we've had the pleasure of meeting." She stood from her throne and offered her hand. "Tiger Lily, Fae Princess of the Ninth Realm Descendant of the Divine."

"Forgive me for my forwardness, Princess. I am Katherine Hawkins." She bowed and kissed her hand.

"And what's your business here in Neverland?"

"I'm here with James."

"*With* Jas?"

"With James—yes," Katherine corrected. A touch of jealousy in her voice.

"This business is between *Jas* and me. Why don't you explore the village with the rest of the crew while we discuss the matter at hand." She waved dismissively towards the door.

"Katherine stays with me. There is nothing we'll discuss that she can't be privy to."

"Quite attached, I see. If she must stay, I'll expect her to remain silent. She'll have no bearing on my decisions."

"You'll have her respect, Princess." I turned to look at Katherine, pleading with my eyes that she honor Tiger Lily's request.

"What is this notion you have about kidnapping Lost Boys?"

"As Katherine said, Peter is effectively killing off his Lost Boys as they age past what he deems appropriate. I'm merely trying to help those less fortunate than me."

"Killing Lost Boys?" she laughed. "He is simply taking them back from where they came."

"Yes, Princess. But in doing so, he leaves them helpless in a society they cannot survive in. Our realm is not like Neverland. It's not kind to their youth. And we have reason to believe that he may be slaughtering them as well."

"So, in lieu of an untimely death, you want my guard to kidnap them and deliver them to your crew?"

"Kidnap is such a harsh word, Princess. I'm simply offering them an alternative to death. As a member of my crew, they can live out the rest of their lives without the weight of Peter's rules."

"As pirates?" she chuckled.

"Precisely."

"Under *your* rule?"

I simply smiled. The irony wasn't lost on me.

"Peter Pan's affairs are governed by the Divine. It's not my place to interfere. I cannot partake in your endeavors." Her words were curt. "However, I can turn a blind eye. That is... if you can help me." Her brow raised as a smile crept across her face. "I need a scapegoat. Someone to blame for any… misfortunes I might cause."

I thought for a moment before responding. "That's a heavy request, Princess. I'd be more likely to accept your offer if you could sweeten the deal."

"I'm listening." She leaned in closer, sitting at the edge of her throne. What was she scheming? It had to be something unsavory to require a scapegoat.

"As you know, Neverland has a way of stealing your memories. I find myself losing touch with my past, and that I cannot make peace with. You are a powerful nymph, a Divine Chosen. Surely you know of a way to stop it."

Tiger Lily sat for a moment; her eyes focused on the corner of her dais. Her lingering silence crushed any hope I had for a solution.

"There is a way." The tone of her voice deepened as she stared into my eyes. "It will cause you to remember every moment of your life in great detail. The good and the bad."

"Yes. That is what I want. To *never* forget."

"Forgetting is often a merciful alternative. You should not want to live in the past, Jas. Neverland simply takes that which does not serve you."

"What serves me is none of your concern, Princess. Just as why you would have need for a scapegoat, is none of mine. Do this for me, and I'll accept your offer."

"You will need to be permanently marked with a talisman. Once it's finished, it cannot be undone."

"Perfect. That's exactly what I was hoping for." Neverland would never be able to dull my hatred for Pan.

Tiger Lily extended her hand. "It appears we have an accord."

"Are you sure you want to do this?" Kat asked while the Princess was busy chanting over several bowls of colored ink.

"It's the only way, Katherine. You'll not sway my choice."

"You don't even know what this ritual entails. Magic always comes at a price. What if—"

"We will speak of it no more. I have decided." Katherine was visibly upset, but I simply could not risk losing my memories. We had only been in Neverland for a short time and already the finer details of my past were becoming fuzzy. I never wanted to forget what Peter had done to me. How he destroyed my life and turned me into a madman obsessed with vengeance.

Tiger Lily poured a circle of salt around two pillows on the floor just below her dais and motioned for me to sit in front of her. "Jas, it is time. Remove your shirt and join me in this sacred space. Let us bind your memories." With the flick of her wrist, candles all around the room ignited, casting us in a warm, flickering glow. She inched closer until our knees touched, gazing intently into my eyes. Tiger Lily reached for my chest, placing her warm palm over my racing heart.

"Are you sure?" she asked one last time. "You should know before we proceed—this will hurt."

I simply nodded my understanding and focused my thoughts on a future without Pan. Nothing could change my mind.

"Let us begin." She drew a raven's claw from her belt and reached for my right forearm. "What is this?" Tiger Lily asked, skimming her delicate fingers across the brand Edward had marked me with.

"It's nothing more than a meaningless scar now. Pay it no mind."

Her eyes met mine, searching for any sign of uncertainty. "It will be covered once we are done."

"And I said to pay it no mind." I'd be damned if I let Blackbeard fuck with my life yet again. I should have flayed his brand from my skin years ago.

"As you wish." Tiger Lily took a deep, centering breath and began again. "Blood and bone," she spoke the words while simultaneously slicing the razor-sharp claw down from the crook of my elbow to my wrist. I groaned at the searing pain. "Ink and skin," she said, pouring the colored bowls she had enchanted only moments ago over my now bleeding wound. "Memories held within." Tiger Lily's eyes rolled back, and her head followed suit, flopping back at an unnatural angle. Her arms seemed to move of their own accord. With the raven's claw still in hand, she began to draw. The sharp point dug into my skin painfully, pooling in a mess of color and blood. "In skin and soul, let them entwine. This is his will; hear me, Divine." The raven's claw dropped from her grasp, echoing around us in the deafening silence. Tiger Lily's head returned to its normal position.

Excruciating pain consumed me as memories flooded my mind. My birth, my parents, the night Peter first took me to Neverland, the first time I tried to fly with faerie dust. Everything I had previously forgotten came crashing down as my life flashed before my eyes. The searing pain in my head was unbearable, like my skull was about to split in two. Surely, I was about to die in agony. It all became too much, and I collapsed into Tiger Lily's arms.

"So shall it be." An otherworldly voice spoke, and I couldn't be sure if it were all in my head as I sunk deeper into the abyss, darkness consuming me.

"JAS," Tiger Lily whispered, stroking my forehead. My head was cradled in her lap, and I was laid out before her.

Katherine tenderly wiped the tears from my eyes while holding my hand, concern plastered on her face.

"It is done." Tiger Lily sprinkled faerie dust over the bloody mess of my forearm before wiping it clean.

There, emblazoned on my arm, obscuring Edward's brand, was a beautifully animated tattoo. A grotesque anatomical heart. The aubergine and crimson muscle was encased in root-like arteries that sprouted out the top like some kind of visceral tree. Three swords pierced the vessel, a visual representation of the past, present, and future. Dripping from the center sword, in time with the beating of my own heart, was a drop of aubergine-colored blood.

"As long as your heart beats, the enchantment will hold fast. Your memories are now sewn permanently into the very fabric of your soul."

"James, are you okay? You passed out." Kat turned to Tiger Lily. "Can we please get him something to drink?"

"Katherine, I'm fine. Just a little...disoriented." I sat up, pinching the bridge of my nose. My head hurt, and my heart ached. I hadn't taken into consideration how much of my childhood I had forgotten during the countless years I'd spent in Neverland. How much those memories would affect me here, now. I needed to dull their rawness and get my focus back on Peter. We still had a mission to accomplish before we left the village and Tiger Lily had made it effortless. "Maybe some mead... to clear my head?"

Katherine squeezed my hand in acknowledgment, keeping her face stoic.

"Guard!" Tiger Lily called out as she stood, straightening out her clothing. "Get Jas a bottle of my finest mead and see them on their way." She reached for my hand and helped pull me to my feet. "Please forgive my quick exit. I have obligations on which to attend."

"Thank you, Princess. I'm at your service, shall the need arise."

"You haven't said much about what happened today." Katherine pushed as she added exactly five drops of the chartreuse poison to the bottle of Tiger Lily's mead.

"What do you want me to say? It wasn't exactly a pleasant experience. I relived every single moment of my life in a matter of mere minutes. I had forgotten the entirety of my childhood while here in Neverland for the first time. I didn't even realize those memories were gone."

"Did you remember things you would have preferred stayed lost?"

"Life is difficult and often shrouded in shadows, Katherine. You know this all too well yourself. But we must seek our darkness and revel in it, or we'll never know where to shine the light. My journey has never been an easy one. It's molded me into the man I am today. I will never regret my decision to protect my memories."

"So... do you still want to deliver this bottle to Peter?"

I laughed maniacally. "Are you serious? Do you think I remembered something that would change my mind?"

"I mean, I guess it is possible that a memory shifted your thoughts."

"I won't rest until that ungrateful little shit is dead."

"Do you think she fancies you?" Kat asked, completely changing the subject.

I couldn't help but chuckle. "Are you jealous? Of Tiger Lily?"

"I'm not jealous."

"Are you sure about that?"

"She seemed awfully comfortable eyeing your 'grown' physique, is all."

I couldn't believe what I was hearing, and I loved it. "Tiger Lily does not interest me." I made my way over to her, hugging her from behind and nuzzling in by her ear. My love for you is like no other." I allowed my hands to wander over her delicious curves. "I only have eyes for you."

Katherine spun around to face me. "This," she grabbed my cock, "belongs to me. Only me."

I growled at her possessiveness, and my cock stirred in

appreciation. "Yes, it does. Shall we take it out and play with it?"

Katherine smiled. "I think we should deliver this mead to Peter before he consumes any more of our time together. When we return, I'll remind you of why your cock loves me, too."

CHAPTER ELEVEN
-CONSUMED-
Katherine

It felt like I might wear a permanent path on the wooden floors of our cabin. My mind was racing, and the pacing gave me an outlet. My skin crawled as my thoughts darted from one thing to the next. The entirety of my life's decisions flickered in my mind like bolts of lightning.

James had left at dawn, leaving me alone again to play victim to my overactive mind. His planning and plotting were barely enough to satiate his hunger for revenge. We were both nearing a breaking point. At least he'd finally slept solidly for the first time in days. Secure in the knowledge that his memories would never fade. It seemed more like a curse than a gift to me. Some things were meant to remain solidly in the dark corners of your psyche.

Yesterday's meeting with the young princess had left a bad taste in my mouth. I saw the way she looked at him. Like James was her next great conquest. He was too consumed with his own vendetta to see it.

I stopped my pacing long enough to pull my wild hair into a messy bun on top of my head. Even the way it clung to me in the heat of the day was irritating. A rush of cool air on the back of my neck was a welcomed relief on my heated skin. It wasn't the temperature that had me burning. It was that girl. Tiger Lily, a seemingly innocent young woman, radiated a nauseating power. I didn't need to touch her to know that her destiny had the potential to upend everything in this realm. How James fit into her overarching plan is what worried me. Because simple favors now meant nothing to her in the scheme of things. The way her fingers had lingered too long on his body. Her coquettish smiles and suggestive looks had gotten under my skin. She looked no more than fifteen, but if she were like Peter, she could be several times my senior. The jealousy was irrational, but it existed, nonetheless.

James' quest for vengeance was becoming increasingly complicated, tangling me into his ever-evolving web. As much as I tried to deny it, James had made it abundantly clear that no matter how much he loved me, that would never be enough. Not while Peter Pan still drew breath. And that undeniable truth broke my heart.

There had been no word, no news that the faerie mead had found its mark. For a poison that could take a life in a matter of moments, it was taking an awfully long time to produce any results. Were all my efforts wasted?

Against my will, my life now revolved around James' vendetta, and this capricious child was at the center of it all. That was the crux I struggled with. A constant battle raged in my head. Could I be complicit in killing a child in the name of love? James insisted that despite his outward appearance, Peter had lived many lifetimes. But I couldn't wipe the youthful sight of him from my conscience. All of this was wrong. I gnawed on my lower lip. Indecision eating me alive. My eyes caught on the tiny vial that contained the last remnants of the poison I'd made. It sat innocuously on the center table, like the essence of springtime captured in a bottle. Its bright, cheery color belying its deadly properties. A wolf in sheep's clothing. A sinister elixir that had the potential to give me everything I ever wanted.

"Are you quite done sulking?" Meadow chimed in from her little cage. "I'm the melancholy one, remember? Besides, it doesn't look good on you."

"I'm fine, Meadow. I just need to think. I need to… I have to…" The answers still eluded me. I couldn't see my next step forward, and the uncertainty left a knot in the pit of my stomach.

"Don't think. Act. That's how pixies do it."

"It's not that simple."

"Yes, it is. What are you feeling right now?"

"So many things."

She gave me a questioning look. "That's your problem. Focus on one emotion. The one that takes up the most space."

I searched within myself, letting my emotions run wild and waited to see which one came out the winner. "Anger," I whispered.

"A useful emotion, that one. Do you like feeling that way?"

"Not particularly."

"Well then, use it to make the change you want. It's that despicable Captain, isn't it? You want to make him happy?"

"He is a good man, Meadow. I know you cannot see it, but he is. And yes, I want to make him happy. Making him happy makes me happy."

"So, stop thinking about things. Take all that bottled-up anger and do something with it."

She was right. I could sit here and contemplate my future for an eternity; all the while, the present was passing me by. I wanted a life with James. Only one thing stood in my way. I grabbed the pistol James had given me. Fuck the poison. I was done waiting. It was time to take fate into my own hands.

MEADOW PROVED INVALUABLE. She was a wealth of knowledge from her little cage attached to my belt. Dictating directions and spouting off Neverland's history. She helped me navigate the island with ease. She even knew all the spots where Peter and his Lost Boys frequented.

I got caught up in the beauty of Neverland. It was breathtaking. Far surpassing that of our realm. Likely because this place hadn't been tainted with bad memories. At least not yet. For a time, I lost the edge of anger that had spurred me into leaving the Jolly Roger behind. I'd been ready to serve Peter's head on a silver platter to my love. But now I hoped we never found him.

"What's that place up there?" I asked, pointing to an ivory tower nestled on a lofty peak in the distance. The afternoon sun glinted off its pristine walls.

"Oh, that's the Temple Mount."

"Maybe you could elaborate a little?"

"It's the house of the Divine. A sanctuary for all those who serve. A place of great power and knowledge."

"What kind of knowledge? Things about the island?"

"Some of it, yes. But there's so much more. An entire library of arcane books. Hidden mysteries of the realms. Magic and prophecies."

This piqued my interest. There was so much that I didn't know about this realm and those beyond. My knowledge of the cosmos was infantile, and I was eager to learn. Possibly, there were books about the Heart of the Divine kept in their collection. James had chosen to stash it away and use it as little as possible. Starkey's warnings of retribution and maintaining balance hadn't sat well with him. But if I had access to those books, I could look for a way to skirt around the rules.

"Can you take me there sometime?"

"You're a funny mortal," she giggled.

"I'm serious. Maybe we could arrange a deal. A little flying time outside the cage, perhaps?"

"Hmm," she hummed to herself as she thoroughly contemplated my offer. "Throw in some Lush tea, and you have a deal."

"Lush tea?"

"Yes. Porthos loves— I mean, loved Lush tea," she said, a slight hitch in her voice as she mentioned her lost mate.

"Whatever it is, I'll get some for you."

"You'll owe me much more than that by the time we're done today. Listen, can't you hear them?"

I hadn't heard anything over the sound of my own feet. I stilled, focusing until the laughter of children drifted in on the breeze.

"We're nearing the Lagoon. The Lost Boys can't resist pestering the mermaids. They make a sport of it." Meadow informed me, but I was barely paying attention. I'd finally found the Lost Boys, and unlike Meadow and her single emotion, fear and excitement were warring within me. My resolve was the only thing that kept me placing one foot in front of the other. I needed to move forward—my conscience be damned.

I hid behind the last wayward palm tree at the edge of the pristine beach. Three young boys swam in the lagoon. All of them focused on whatever rambunctious game they were playing. They all seemed accounted for, except the one I was looking for.

"I don't see Peter. These *are* his Lost Boys, so he can't be far, right?"

"His pixie told me there's a hidden grotto he likes to visit to get away from the others."

"Yes, yes, I know the place. You think he's there?"

"Would be a perfect coincidence if he is. Peter Pan without his Lost Boys—that would make your job much easier."

"You do realize that I intend to kill him, right?"

"Just because I'm a pixie doesn't mean that I'm simple. It's not like you've tried to hide your intentions."

"And you're okay with this?"

She shrugged her shoulders in response. "Pixies die all the time. It's the natural way of things. You live for a time and then return to the Divine. Unless you're Porthos... my poor, sweet Porthos." Her beautiful tinkling of bells became a soft weeping. Now was not the time to deal with Meadow's heartache, and I took it as my sign to quit stalling and get on with it.

"Wait here, Meadow. I'll come back for you."

"Not like I'm going anywhere," she snorted, wiping away her tears and motioning at her cage. Her words were thick with emotion, laced with some clear indignation. I brushed her off. Her imprisonment was yet another decision that I was still trying to justify to myself. But I could only deal with one lapse in judgment at a time. I hid her cage among the foliage before I took a shaky step toward fulfilling my destiny.

I pulled the pistol from the belt at my waist and did my best to remain hidden as I made my way to the cliffs. Luck was on my side. I managed to arrive at the small crevice in the rock wall without attracting attention from Peter's Lost Boys.

It took a moment for my eyes to adjust to the dim light of the grotto. But there, resting before the pristine pool, was Peter. Curled up on a fur. A lock of auburn hair fell across cheeks dotted with freckles. He looked every bit the innocent child as he slept. A tear escaped from the corner of my eye as I brought the pistol up, aiming at the slight rise and fall of his chest. My hand shook violently. My whole body was at war with itself. One flinch of a muscle and the trigger would be pulled. And I wouldn't have to share James with this boy anymore.

But I couldn't do it.

I sank to my knees, a sob escaping my lips, echoing off the cavern walls. I'd been so close to achieving my destiny, and I couldn't do it. The sound of my breakdown had the boy instantly on his feet with his sword drawn.

He cocked his head as intelligent eyes took me in. "I remember you. You're awfully pretty to be Jas' mother."

"No, I'm not his mother. I'm his, err... wife." I'm not sure why I referred to myself as his wife. I tried to reason that it was easier than describing the intricacies of our relationship to a child. But saying it aloud brought a flush to my cheeks and a longing in my heart.

"Only old men have wives—I suppose it makes sense for Jas. But are you sure you really want to be a wife? That's just another name for a housemaid. Do the laundry, cook the meals, and clean the house. That doesn't sound like much fun," he said as he sheathed his sword, obviously deeming that I was no threat to him, even with my pistol hanging useless in my hand. "But I've got an idea! Come and be our mother," he said, a spark of light flickering in his brown eyes. "You could tell us stories, sing us to sleep at night, and in return, we'd build you a house and bring you flowers all the time."

My words caught in my throat. How was it this boy had reached into my soul, dragging out things I didn't even know I wanted for myself. A vision of a blonde-haired little boy playing in a field danced through my mind. The possibility of having a child with James was something I hadn't allowed myself to consider. A figment of a reality that was slowly slipping through my fingers.

"That sounds lovely," I choked out. I took a tentative step toward him. If I could only touch him. Then, I could see what his future held. "Do you think the other boys would enjoy having a mother?"

"Doesn't matter what they think. I'm the captain, so whatever I say goes."

I was so close to him now. I could have easily raised my pistol and shot him at close range before he even had a chance to react. But instead of a pistol, I reached for him, cupping his cheek, and letting the vision flood into me.

An open window.

A beautiful woman crying.

A line in the sand.

Tiger Lily.

Bones—so many bones.

A crocodile snapping its jaws.

Blood spreading over ivory silk.

James.

I recoiled from him as if I'd touched an ember, trying to mask the sharp intake of air. His eyes narrowed, letting me know he hadn't missed the change in my behavior.

"Are you fae?" he asked, appraising me with new eyes.

"No, I'm not fae. I'm human, like you."

"You may be mortal, but you're more than human. You're special."

I laughed at that. "Well, I'm glad you think I'm special. Does 'special' still fit the bill for a good mother?"

"That means you're *extra* qualified. What do you say? Are you ready to leave Granddad behind and join the Lost Boys?"

"Granddad?" I chuckled at his depiction of James. "I thought once a Lost Boy, always a Lost Boy? Why can't you and Jas settle your issues and let it go?"

"Nah, Jas broke the rules. He should have stayed gone, but now he's made it personal. To be honest, I can barely remember our time together. But as long as he remains on the island, he's my enemy. It's that simple."

"Simple would be for both of you to forget about all of this and go on with your own lives."

"That's not the way of things. But we'll teach you all the rules once you've agreed to be our mum. So, what do you say?"

"I'm sorry, Peter, but I can't be your mother. I can't even be a good wife."

Chapter Twelve
-MADNESS-
James

Frustration gnawed at me. Katherine's poisoned mead still hadn't proven effective. The bastard was still roaming the damn island, eluding my wrath like some kind of specter, able to appear and disappear at a moment's thought. I lit a cigar and focused on the map. Where would I hide if I were a young cocksure prick?

Katherine opened the door, standing silently in the entryway. She'd been missing all afternoon. She knew I'd be upset. I could feel the guilt radiating off her slight frame.

"I'm going to take Meadow away from you if you don't

stop sneaking off without leaving word. I've already told you my feelings on the matter. If something happens to you, your little pixie will pay the ultimate price," I chided, keeping my eyes focused on the map of Neverland.

I hated having to reprimand her, but she was going to get herself killed running off alone. It was a thought I didn't want to entertain. She was my anchor, keeping me tethered to the last bits of my sanity. Without her, I had nothing but vengeance and venom running through my veins. She was the light in my darkness.

Katherine stared at me, her eyes red and damp. Her chin quivering. Something was wrong.

"Love? Why are you crying? I'm simply trying to keep you safe."

"I'm... I'm—" An outburst of sobbing cut her words short.

"Are you having one of your womanly moments?"

"I'm a horrible wife."

"Wife?" I'd seen Katherine upset before, but this was some kind of madness. I pushed the bottle of rum towards her, urging her to drink.

"Us... we keep fighting, and then that bitch, Tiger Lily, I don't like her. And the stupid poisoned mead..." she rambled as the tears continued to fall.

"Katherine, what happened today? Do I need to kill someone?"

"That's exactly the problem, James, I couldn't even kill him when I had the chance."

She had gone off the deep end. Between the sobbing

and mad rambling, I was beginning to fear the worst. Fits of hysteria weren't uncommon among women her age. Either that, or she'd been poisoned. Something was very wrong.

"Kill who, Katherine? Who were you trying to kill?"

She dropped her head, wringing her wrists and staring at the ground. "Peter."

"I'm sorry, did you say *Peter*?" I must have misheard. I lifted her chin, catching her gaze. "Did you run into Peter fucking Pan today?" Anger crept up like a dark grey mist rolling in, obscuring a calm sea beneath it.

"I... I... James, your eyes. They just flashed red."

"Never mind my eyes," I said, dismissing her delusions. I wasn't about to let her change the subject. "Did you see Peter today?"

"I thought if I could just finish him, once and for all, we could be happy. Just the two of us. I brought my pistol. He was sound asleep. It should have been easy. But I couldn't, James, I couldn't pull the trigger." Her eyes welled up again.

"Why don't you tell me exactly what happened today?" I tried to conceal my anger. If I wanted answers, I was going to have to stay calm.

"I took Meadow in search of Peter. Like I said, I just wanted it all to end. We found him sleeping in the grotto. I had the perfect opportunity. He would have been none the wiser," she shook her head, "I froze. I couldn't kill a sleeping babe." More sobbing interrupted her story. "I can't even fulfill my own destiny."

"It's not your destiny to fulfill, Katherine. I don't need you to fight my battles," I sighed. "What happened next?"

"My crying roused him. He remembered me, James. He thought I was your mother."

This made me laugh. "My mother?"

"Yes," she huffed. "I told him I was your wife."

"My wife?" I had never really considered marriage before. Katherine referring to herself as my wife, even though we lived as such without the title, felt somehow foreign.

"I didn't know how else to put it. I wasn't about to teach the boy how relationships work."

"He's hundreds of years old, Kat."

"Well, he looks like a child. It's unsettling." She paused, rubbing her heart. "He asked me to be his mother. To tell them stories and sing to them. James, I know what it's like to lose your mom. To crave that unconditional love."

"Pish," I dismissed her comments. Peter didn't deserve her empathy. "Nothing has changed. He's been looking for a 'mother' since the day we met." I often wondered why he was forever searching for a mother when he chose to leave his actual mum for Neverland.

"I was able to—" A loud knock at the door startled Katherine.

"Yes, what is it?"

"Captain, forgive my interruption." Smee smiled as he entered the cabin. "The gnomes have delivered a package for you."

"Ah, yes. Please, bring it here. I've been expecting its arrival. Thank you, Smee. You may show yourself out."

"Aye, Captain."

"Perfect timing. I commissioned a gift for you." I offered Kat the box, a smile spread across her tear-soaked face.

"For me?" she asked, surprised.

"Yes, it dawned on me that I haven't been the best... husband." Katherine's eyes lit up.

"Go ahead, kitten, open it. I'm dying to see it myself."

Kat slowly opened the box. "Um." Her head tilted to the side, and her lips pursed.

"Well? What do you think?"

"What is it?" she asked, staring into the box awkwardly.

"According to Smee, the gnomes, who are mostly tailors, are quite the tradesmen when they aren't tailoring. He said there was nothing they couldn't make. By the look on your face, he was right."

"But what exactly is it?" she asked again, pulling it from the box. "It's jiggly," she said, giggling. "Is it... it looks like a tentacle?"

"Indeed." I smiled. The gnomes had outdone themselves. The toy was perfect. A burnt orange replica of the real thing. There were knobby suckers all along the underside. While the delicate tip grew quickly in girth, promising a delectable stretch. I was eager to use it on her. "Since our escape from the Kraken, I've been having dreams about you being ravished by one of its massive tentacles. You seem to enjoy it greatly. I figured, why not appease my subconscious mind? I want to see you squirm in the flesh."

"James, I… I don't know?"

"Oh, don't play coy, little kitten. We both know you'll like it."

"I've never. I don't even know what to say."

"Why, Miss Hawkins, are you worried about what polite society would say if you were sexually aroused by a—*gasp* —girthy tentacle?"

Katherine blushed, and I knew at that moment she was intrigued. Even if she didn't want to admit it. Her body gave her away. "It's not about what society thinks, James. It's simply just strange. I've had a horribly heavy day. I need to clear my head. Thank you for the gift. I think I'm going to draw a bit before bed."

"Why don't I make you some tea? It will help you relax."

"I would love that. Thank you."

WHEN I RETURNED to our cabin, Kat was scribbling furiously by the window. Lost in her drawings. "Here's some tea, love. Why don't you take a moment and share a drink with me?"

"Thank you," she said, blowing the steam from the cup.

"What exactly is that creature you are drawing?" I asked, eyeing the beast that was taking shape on the canvas.

"It's a crocodile. I saw one in my visions. It's been haunting my mind. Does Neverland have crocodiles?"

"I know of at least one. I've only seen it a few times. It's nothing to fear."

"Hmm." She paused for a moment before taking a sip. "This tea is delicious. It almost tastes like sassafras. What is it?"

"It's a ceremonial tea among the Neverlanders. They call it *Lush*." I watched as Kat sipped deeply on her cup, knowing exactly what was about to happen.

"Lush, that's the tea Meadow asked me for. She said her mate, Porthos, loved Lush tea."

"I'm sure he did," I chuckled. "It's often reserved for special occasions." Lush tea was a potent aphrodisiac used to help enhance sexual experiences and connection. It makes one feel… amazing.

"And what makes this a special occasion?"

"Simply having you home safe after a run-in with Pan is reason enough to celebrate." I placed a chaste kiss on her cheek. "I love you, Katherine Hawkins. Please don't attempt to kill Peter Pan without me ever again. I'd be lost without you."

"Do you feel that?" Her lips parted, and a gentle sigh escaped.

"Feel what, love?"

"The way the ship sways with the sea. It's as though they are one. Close your eyes." She stood up and walked to the large window. "Do you feel it?" she asked, again swaying her hips with the gentle rocking.

The Lush was beginning to take hold. It wouldn't be long before she'd be begging for my touch. I closed in on her, pressing myself against her undulating back, and wrapped my hands around her tiny waist. Breathing in her delectable scent, I placed a gentle kiss atop her shoulder. "You smell divine." I trailed my tongue up along her neck, stopping just below her ear. "You taste even better."

Katherine hummed in approval, gripping the back of my head and rousing my cock.

"Tell me, kitten." I ran my hands over her breasts. "Are you still focused on the sway of the ship?"

Kat's breath hitched as I dipped a finger under her stays, finding her pebbled nipple. "James, what was in that tea? My head is spinning."

"It's just what Lush does, love. Don't be afraid of it. Let the feeling take over."

"I want to feel… everything." She writhed, tugging at her clothes. "The air. The sway of the ship. Your hands. Help me get my stays off."

"Say no more." I wasted no time. I pulled my dagger and sliced up the back of her laces, freeing her from the confines of her clothing. She had never looked more beautiful. I was feeling the Lush myself. The scent of her drove a primal need. I wanted to taste every inch of her nakedness. I wanted to dominate her tiny frame. Make her scream my name in the throes of ecstasy.

Katherine spun around to face me. I reached for her,

pulling her in and kissing her hard. I let my tongue take over and explore her sinful mouth. She met me with a moan and kissed me back with fervor. It was as if we had never really kissed before. She was the air I needed to survive, and all this time, I'd been suffocating.

I wanted more. I needed to consume her, fill her, and the Lush would not let me wait. I reluctantly pulled away, ripping my shirt from my body. The air swirled around me, and I mindlessly caressed my own chest. My nipples were hard and seeking touch, much like the rest of my body. I wanted to watch her squirm while I defiled her, and that desire consumed my mind.

I quickly scanned the room, stopping at the full-length mirror. I grabbed a chair and dragged it in front of the looking glass, angling it so whoever sat in it would have a close-up view of themselves. "Katherine, you'd better run because once I get my hands on you, it's over. I *will have* my way with you." I stalked towards her naked frame. And she squealed, running around the table. My demon loved it when she ran. "The longer it takes for me to catch you, the more ideas I come up with."

Katherine's eyes widened. "Lucky me," she giggled and ran back across the room, effectively cornering herself. I chuckled, grabbing a piece of her disheveled stays and ripped a length of linen from the remnants.

"Enjoying the Lush?" I asked as her hands mindlessly roamed her curves.

"It's intoxicating. Everything's so... carnal. I can feel the air around me."

"Come here, kitty, kitty."

"You want me?" She looked at me through her lashes and bit her lip. "Come get me."

"Done," I growled. My demon purred as I slowly stalked closer. Closing in on our meek prey.

"James, your eyes, they're red again."

"All the better to see you with, my dear."

Katherine screamed as I darted across the room. Her fear intoxicated the predator within me. I had her trapped. Grabbing her by the waist, I hauled her over my shoulder, slapping her ass and squeezing hard, drawing out a moan of approval. I grabbed the boxed tentacle from the table and made my way over to the chair.

"James—"

"Shhh, let the Lush soothe your fears. Give in to the sensation."

I placed Kat in front of me and sat in the chair. Her perfect ass reflected in the mirror. A blossoming red welt in the shape of my hand was spreading across her cheek. "Close your eyes and focus on what you feel." I dragged the torn linen across her body, swirling the fabric around her breasts. Goose bumps erupted along her porcelain skin, and she purred. I allowed it to catch along her nipples, teasing them with a soft flick.

She started to sway again in a speechless demand for more as her body chased the linen's caress.

I slid my hands down her arms, wrapping the fabric over her wrists, securing them tightly, and spun her around to face the mirror. "Open your eyes. Do you see how beautiful you look bound before me?"

She hesitated for a moment before relaxing into herself and relishing in her reflection. I circled her waist, allowing my hands to explore the soft curve of her belly. Standing up, watching her intently, I slid my hands up her sides, encouraging her to lift her arms, and hooked her bound hands behind my head. The gentle arch in her spine pushed her breasts forward, displaying them in the most erotic way.

"Your body is a masterpiece," I whispered into her ear while cupping her breasts and pinching her taught nipples.

Katherine let out a heavy breath.

"Did you like that?"

"Mmhm, do it again."

I circled her breasts, denying her request, barely touching her skin.

"Please." She arched her back farther, begging.

I couldn't deny her any longer. I ran my tongue along the shell of her ear and rolled her nipples between my fingers, deepening the pinch.

She moaned, instinctively pulling away from the pain, and my cock twitched with excitement. I reached for my breaches, loosening the ties, and freeing myself. "I wanna show you just how pretty your flower looks when you're excited." I pulled Kat down on my lap, reclining her back against my chest. Lifting her legs, one at a time, I draped them over the arms of the chair. Reaching between her thighs, I pushed them farther apart, spreading her wide and exposing every inch of her glistening slit. "Look at how beautiful you bloom for me. Spread wide and dripping with need."

"Touch me, please, James. I ache for you."

I reached between her legs, gliding my fingers over her slick skin. Katherine groaned at my touch, throwing her head back on my shoulder and biting her lip. Her body tensed as her legs pushed against the arms of the chair, straining for more friction, spreading herself even wider. I circled her clit ever-so-gently teasing the delicate bud. Her breathing had become panting, and her thighs began to tremble.

"You like that, don't you, kitty Kat?" She didn't answer, but the look on her face told me everything I needed. I removed my hand from her clit and sampled her sweet nectar. "You taste so good. You're so wet and ready for me." I reached under the chair, grabbing the tentacle. "Now, be a good girl, and let me take care of you." My cock was rock hard and throbbing with excitement. I slid the knobby toy slowly through her wetness, coating it in her arousal. The sensation of that alone had her writhing on my lap.

"James," she protested between mews of pleasure.

"What's your safe word, kitten?" I continued sliding the toy delicately through her folds, giving her time to get used to the foreign sensations.

"Poison," she breathed out the word, bringing a sinister smile to my lips.

Once she relaxed back into me, I inserted the tip of the tentacle, teasing her opening slowly before sliding it past the first set of thick suckers.

Katherine gasped.

"That's my good girl. Let's see how much you can take?" I slowly pushed past the next two sets, watching in the looking glass as her tight pussy stretched to accommodate the growing girth. I paused, giving her a moment to adjust, and twisted the tentacle, drawing out the most animalistic groan from Kat I had ever heard. She was loving it, lost in the sensation, and it was driving me wild. "Shall we try a bit more?"

"Yes, please," she groaned.

I pushed up to the edge of the next row of suckers. "Don't hold your breath, beautiful. Breathe. That's it. You take it so well." She pulled in a deep breath, and as she exhaled, I pushed past another row of ridged suckers. Her opening stretched to the brink as she cried out in painful pleasure. I reached for her clit and circled her bud. Her body began to tremble. Within mere moments, she was falling over the edge into an explosive orgasm. Her hips grinding in my lap, riding out her pleasure on the tentacle, just like I had dreamed she would. It was a beautiful sight. Her nipples peaked, a blush forming along her cheeks, and her mouth agape, moaning like a cat in heat.

Watching alone was almost enough to take me with her. My cock begged for release. I slid the tentacle out, lifted her ass off my lap, and seated her back on my cock, burring myself to the root in her dripping wet pussy. "Fuuck, Katherine," I growled in her ear. "I could watch you take my cock all day." Our reflection in the looking glass was pure debauchery. We were lost in the moment. Consumed with pleasure. I pumped my hips against her bucking frame. Her pussy gripped my cock tightly as she fell into another orgasm. Her core pulsing with pleasure pushed me over the edge into ecstasy. I quickly came undone, losing myself deep within her.

"You will never fail to astound me, Katherine." I unbound her wrists and cradled her against my chest. Your body was made for my pleasure."

Katherine beamed with the praise. "I love you, James." She smiled, a sweet blush blooming on her cheeks. "And I think I love Lush tea," she giggled. "Thank you for pushing my boundaries. But maybe next time you tell me before drugging me?"

"But then there is no surprise," I chuckled. "I love you too, Kitty Kat." I picked her up and carried her to our bed. "Are you okay? Did I push you too hard?"

"I'm a little sore, but it was worth the pain." She smiled. "You were right about the toy. I loved it."

I kissed her forehead and tucked her in. "Rest, love, you earned it."

"Are you not coming to bed?"

"I'll be there in a moment." I wanted nothing more than

to curl up next to Katherine and fall into a deep sleep. My body and mind were spent and pleasantly satiated. But there was a nagging feeling in the pit of my stomach that someone had been watching our little escapade. I made my way to the window and looked around. Nothing but the rippling waters and starry skies. I reached for the rum, taking a heavy pull to settle my nerves, and joined Katherine in bed.

CHAPTER THIRTEEN
-ARROGANCE-
James

It was that transient time when night shifted into dawn. The witching hour. And even though my body was spent, my mind wouldn't quiet. I found myself staring at the ceiling. A deep-seated fear manifested as a gnawing ache that wouldn't go away, and I rubbed at my chest. I wasn't entirely sure I liked the man I was becoming. Katherine deserved better than a depraved pirate hell-bent on revenge.

By some miracle, I'd found myself a woman who lived in the darkness with me. We were the same. Her line between pleasure and pain was just as blurred as mine. It petrified me to think that one day, I might take it too far.

Katherine was curled into my side. Her breathing was slow and rhythmic against my neck. She'd drifted off after I'd ravaged her in ways I wasn't entirely proud of. I'd allowed my demon out to play. It was happening far too often, and I worried that I would lose control altogether.

The room, with all my mercurial thoughts, felt suffocating. I needed a breath. Maybe the endless sky was just big enough to let these wild thoughts free from my mind. I felt like I was on a collision course with my destiny, and I'd be damned if I let it destroy me while I lay there staring at the ceiling.

I untangled myself from Kat without waking her. Slowly rising from our bed and slinging my baldric over my bare chest. I didn't bother to fully dress, but old habits ensured I'd never be unarmed.

TOPSIDE OFFERED A MUCH-NEEDED REPRIEVE. The cool breeze washed over me, cleansing me from my punishing thoughts. I let out a sigh. The nostalgic smell of salt filled my nostrils. The knot of tension in my chest eased, at least enough that I could pull in a deep breath. Despite my inner turmoil, the night was serene, with the light of a full moon setting the water alight in flickers of silver. At least now I could think clearly. I had to come up with a plan. A real, foolproof plan to settle this debt with Pan once and for all. It was time to move on. I had thought I wanted to revel in this, and maybe my demon still did. But I had to put this vendetta behind me. That's what Katherine needed.

I fished into the pocket of my breeches and pulled out the ruby. I'd been trying to determine how to use it without damning the future I had. One evil deed would be revisited on me threefold. I couldn't welcome that into our lives. But on the flip side, Katherine and I were only one thought away from leaving Neverland for good. We could find ourselves a pristine corner of the cosmos. But would I ever be happy with that? Knowing that Pan got away with everything?

"You're not good enough for her." This time it wasn't the usual hollow voices in my head. It was a voice I knew all too well. *Peter.*

Fuck! I must have really been losing it if Pan's voice had replaced the others. I balled my fists at my temples, pulling at my hair until pain tore through my scalp. Willing the voices to leave me be before I descended into complete madness.

The sound of boots landing on the floorboards behind me brought me back to reality. I whirled at the sound, so distracted that I didn't even pull my sword. My nemesis stood solidly on the deck, for once facing me head-on.

Relief washed over me when I realized Peter was here in the flesh and not a delusion taking up residence in my mind.

"You're not telling me anything I don't already know," I grumbled.

"I saw the things you did to her. Now I know I made the

right decision to cut you out." He spat at me; his face scrunched up in righteous indignation.

"So, it was you who was watching," I said, putting the pieces together.

"You're not a Lost Boy. You're an animal."

"No more than you. You lure boys to paradise with your false promises, and when they no longer serve your purpose, you dispose of them."

"You've been away from Neverland for too long, Jas. You don't know me anymore."

"Oh, I know you. You've been cutting boys from your ranks for years now."

"You don't know anything."

"I've seen them. Heard their stories. Do you remember Eli? He had people who loved him. A father. And you ended all of it."

"He's still here. If his father wants him, I bet he can find his bones moldering in the Viridianwood."

My jaw clenched as his callous admission sunk in. He'd confirmed what I knew all along. Smee's son was dead. "You're a heartless little fuck, aren't you? Do you have any virtue at all?"

"I don't have time for those that break the rules!"

"Haven't you noticed that they all break the rules?" I shouted at him. The thought of all those dead boys, knowing how easily it could have been me, whittled away the fragile hold I had on my temper. Peter's lips set in a hard line; his brows drawn in a scowl. My words obviously penetrated the veiled memories that Neverland kept hidden from him. His jaw worked for a moment, but instead of responding to the accusations I laid at his feet, he attacked at my only weakness.

"Now I see why she came for me."

"She came to finish you off, Peter. She did it for me. Because she loves me. And that's something you've never known."

"No, you have it all wrong, Jas. She is looking for a way out. And after what I just saw, I can't leave her here with you. The Lost Boys and I can give her a better home."

"You've truly lost your mind, Peter," I said, the demon beginning to swell in my chest. My archenemy threatening to make off with my girl; now, *that* was a dangerous cocktail.

"She wants to be a mother. I saw it in her eyes."

The idea of Katherine as a mother gutted me. Every man should want to bury his seed in the woman he loves and watch that love grow into a child. But I was broken. I could never be a father. I could never give her that. In a split second, the vision I had of my future with Kat felt like it might crumble in my hands.

"You don't know anything about her," I shot back at him, trying to sound confident, but the weight of my emotions stuck thick in my throat.

"I think I do, and I'm prepared to fight for her honor. A duel—winner gets the girl."

I laughed at the notion. At first, it sounded absurd, but the laughter quickly shifted into a sinister chuckle. I reached into my pocket, palming the ruby, ready to set my intentions. "It's about time, Peter." The night was instantly charged with possibilities. "But I wish for this to be a fair fight. No flying, no backstabbing."

"Winner gets the girl," he reiterated and spit in his hand, ready to shake on the terms. What he didn't know was that the power of the ruby had already sealed the deal. I'd never agree to give Katherine up, but I didn't plan on losing. I got over myself enough to shake his hand in agreement. A split second later, all manner of niceties were off. I pulled my cutlass from its scabbard and secured the ruby back into my pocket.

I stepped left, and he mirrored me. His short sword glinting in the full moonlight. A distant rumble of thunder rolled across the sea. An ominous tolling as we marched toward our destiny.

He made the first move, coming at me with a direct swing of his blade. His arrogance showed as he thought he could dispatch me with rudimentary swordplay. The clink of steel kissing steel took on a rhythmic sound as we fought. Each of us gained and lost ground as we danced around the deck.

Peter was nimble, even when he wasn't flying. His slight frame darted behind the masts and hurdled over barrels.

"Running from me, Pan?"

"Not running. I'm betting you wear out first so I can finish you off without dinging up my blade." He flashed a devious smile at me, and I saw the excitement in his eyes. This was a game to him. I wished I had that kind of indifference. That my life hadn't revolved around him when he'd all but forgotten about me. But tonight, I would make him feel all the years I suffered.

I watched his every move carefully, biding my time. Eventually, he'd take a wrong step, and I knew this ship like the back of my hand.

I had him right where I wanted. My cutlass was quick, cutting the ropes that held the mainsail with deadly grace. Like a dark premonition, the black banners of the Jolly Roger fell over him, pinning him to the deck. I pounced on his sprawling form, dragging him from the tangle of canvas, and wrapped my arm around his neck.

"Now, this is more like it. How does it feel, Pan? To be helpless?"

"You're a bloody poor sport, mate," he managed to croak out. Still not taking any of this seriously.

"You owe me a life, goddamn you!"

He grunted in my arms, unable to get a word out now that I closed off his airway. A moment of panic set in, paralyzing me. How did I want to finish him off? Like this, where I smothered the life out of him? Or in a pool of blood, with him at the end of my blade? Ling chi? It was a ridiculous time to be contemplating killing methods. But it had to live up to all the years I dreamed of this.

In my momentary distraction, Pan managed to land a solid elbow in my gut. It was enough to loosen my grip, and the little fucker slipped out. He stumbled away from me, regaining his footing, and grabbing his sword. His breath heaved as he rubbed at the red marks on his neck. It was the first time that he had the decency to look afraid.

Thunder cracked, louder this time, and the skies opened. The torrent of rain coming down was as close as the boy would ever come to crying. My demon purred at the thought. The look of fear quickly melted from his eyes, his features contorting into a dark scowl. He made a move to fly, but it was useless, and he stumbled again. The power of the ruby holding firm.

"What the—"

"Trying to cheat already? I knew I couldn't trust you to be honorable."

"What have you done to me?"

"Just making sure you're playing by the rules. You do so love the rules, don't you, Peter?"

The muscles in his jaw ticked, and the thunder crack that followed was deafening. He lunged for me, swinging his sword in one fluid movement. I pulled back a moment before his blade whizzed past my face. A smile crept into the corners of my mouth. I was finally getting to him.

The deck began to fill with onlookers. The last remnants of the Lost Boys he'd tried to dispose of. I wasn't just fighting for myself. This was a battle for all of us.

I put everything I had into that fight. My calculating mind and muscle memory from years of fighting combined to forge me into a lethal weapon. When I pinned him against the mainmast, it was my opportunity to finish it. Our blades locked against one another. His strength pitted against mine, and he was no match for me. I pressed toward him until we were nose to nose, our swords crossed between us, quivering with the combined strain behind them.

"You tried to make me disappear," I whispered, my eyes focusing on his. "Now your ghosts have returned to send you off to hell."

"What have you become, Jas? It looks like the fires of hell burn in your eyes. It's not me that's damned." Instead of fear at his imminent death, the boy looked resolved. Maybe he knew it was over. That his time had finally run out. With a twist of my cutlass, his hand gave out, and his blade clattered to the ground. Now, it was only Peter and the tip of my sword. I was giddy with a lifetime of anticipation, culminating in this very moment. No one would keep me from my vengeance. Not even the Divine.

"James, don't! He's just a boy." Katherine's voice cut through the rain. I had him in my grasp. My life was about to become my own again. But her words tore into my soul.

"She'll never forgive you for this," the voices hissed inside my head, and my sword faltered, hanging uselessly in my hand.

"Please, James. I love you. Don't do this. Come away with me, and we'll forget all about him," she pleaded with me, but she was wrong. I would never forget what he did to me. I'd gone to great lengths to ensure that.

My gaze drifted from Pan as the weight of my next decision threatened to crush me. That moment of hesitation cost me everything.

In a flash, a rain-soaked Peter collided with my sword hand, sending me sprawling. My cutlass clattered to the deck while the ruby dislodged from my pocket and rolled in the opposite direction, leaving me completely unarmed. Pan lunged away from me, diving for his own sword. I was blinded by rage, and the emotion made me reckless. I gained my footing and barreled toward him just as his sword came down in a perfectly timed arc.

I felt the impact before the pain set in. I stumbled past him, my knees hitting the slick planks. Katherine's scream sounded a million miles away as my eyes settled on the stump where my hand had been severed from my body. Instead of bright red, the blood that poured from the wound was a dark aubergine. I stared in disbelief, the contents of my stomach threatening to spill on the deck with my strange blood. What was happening to me? The edges of my vision grew dark. Shock, mixed with searing pain, created a potent cocktail that threatened to drag me under.

"Missing something, Jas?" Peter shouted. I looked up to find him holding my dismembered hand in front of my face. I tried to grab it from him, but he danced away from me, jumping on the railing of the ship.

"Give it back," I ground out through the pain.

"Looks like you've sold your soul, my old friend. What's one missing piece?" he laughed as he took in the unusual color of my blood. "Perfect bait for crocodiles. You know," he taunted nonchalantly as if he wasn't holding the lifeless remains of my hand, "they troll these waters for any sign of an easy meal, and they can smell when blood is spilled—especially your kind." He held my hand over the railing, letting the aubergine blood drip into the sea below. "I have a feeling you're tastier than most."

My mind was in chaos, but I didn't miss the sound of splashing water and the snapping of teeth below deck. I staggered to my feet, my injured arm pinned to my chest, the dark blood staining my shirt. I took a step toward him on shaky legs. Pan smirked at me and tossed my severed hand overboard as if he were discarding a piece of trash.

"No!" A guttural scream poured from my lips. I stumbled the rest of the way, the railing catching me in the gut. It was too late, and the only thing left of my hand... of my pride, was now in the belly of the enormous beast. The spines of the crocodile slashed through the dark water, still looking for more.

Pan's sword sunk into the railing only inches from me, shaking me from the shock and bringing me back to the present danger I was in.

"If I have to, I'll take you one piece at a time until I've won the duel, and I walk away with a new mother."

I couldn't bring myself to move. I was beaten. I wasn't even a whole man. It was time to welcome death. It seemed like a peaceful adventure at that moment. I closed my eyes and turned my face up to the falling rain. Ready to accept my fate.

The sound of a gunshot echoed in my ears, startling me, and my eyes popped open. Katherine stood beside me. In one hand, she clutched the ruby; in the other, her smoking pistol pointed at the sky. A goddess in her righteous fury. The rain plastered her white shift to her body, and the wind whipped her hair around her face. The sight of her was all that held me together.

"Take one more step toward him, and I'll reconsider sparing you," she shouted. Cocking the pistol and pointing it at Peter. "The duel is over. I'm choosing to stay with James. Now, get the fuck off this ship!" she shrieked, firing off another round into the sky. The Heart of the Divine obeyed Katherine's commands, ending the fight and the rules that bound us. A bewildered Pan took to the air, flying off toward the mainland.

CHAPTER FOURTEEN
-BLOOD-

James

The moment Pan took flight, Katherine knelt beside me. "James!" She grabbed my wrist and raised it high above my head, panic trembling through her body. "Keep your arm up. We must stop the bleeding." She ripped at her shift, wadding up the fabric and pressing it firmly against the bloody stump. Scorching, white-hot pain ripped through my body.

"Fuck, Katherine! Stop, just stop."

"I'm sorry, James. I'm so sorry. I can't. I have to stop the bleeding."

"Don't bother. I'm ready... to meet my... my demise." I focused on the immense pain. The way the blood felt sticky and warm, spilling down my arm. I deserved every agonizing spark. I'd lost. It was over.

"Smee!" Kat yelled, ignoring me. Straining, she pulled the belt from my waist. "Help me wrap this tourniquet."

"I've never seen blood like this before. We need faerie dust. Miss Hawkins, where's your pixie?" Smee briefly turned his eyes to mine before looking back at the sanguineous mess before him. I must have been a gruesome sight because his face was ghostly white, and he was sweating profusely. "This is going to hurt, Captain. Brace yourself." He wrapped the belt around my arm. His hands were now almost black, coated in my dark purple blood.

"Fuuckk!" I screamed as he tightened the makeshift tourniquet. Pain shot down my arm and through my missing hand. It wasn't there, but I could still feel it. My vision blurred, and the world around me faded in and out of darkness.

"She's in our cabin." Katherine's voice seemed miles away.

"Just let... me..." I pleaded.

"Starkey! Go, find the damn pixie and bring her here. Now!" Smee barked orders, taking the lead.

Why were they ignoring me? There was no need for them to save me. I didn't want to survive. Everything I fought for, everything I endured, it was all for naught. I'd never defeat Pan as half a man. He had won. The bastard had bested me. I closed my eyes and wished for death.

. . .

"HOW LONG SHOULD IT TAKE?" The distant sound of Katherine's voice roused me, bringing back the searing pain and the memory of how I'd failed. I struggled to hear her words, though I could sense her presence beside me.

"It should have worked by now. Give me the damned pixie," Smee demanded. "I'll shake every last drop of dust from her pathetic little frame."

"You'll do no such thing!" Kat snapped back. "Meadow, please. We have to try?"

I heard the buzz of Meadow's wings pass by my ear. "I told you both. Faerie dust can't cure *everything*. More won't change his outcome. At least the bleeding has stopped. If he's lucky, he'll survive."

"Smee…" The word came out as a mere whisper. It was all I could muster. I opened my eyes, blinking away the confusion. I was still splayed out on the deck.

"James!" Katherine grabbed my left hand. "He's awake!" She smiled down at me. Her beautiful face shone like an angel against the cloud-peppered sky. "You're safe. The bleeding has stopped. You're going to be okay. Let me get you some water."

"Where is Smee?"

"I'm here, Captain." Smee's head popped into view.

"Rum," I demanded.

"No need." Katherine squeezed my hand. "I have an elixir—"

"No!" I wouldn't use her magics. My trust in her was wavering. Plus, I didn't want a reprieve from the physical pain. I was a failure. I deserved to feel every gut-wrenching throb. Rum, however, would dull my aching psyche.

"James," she pleaded. "Let me help. I know you are in immense pain."

"Help me to my cabin."

"Captain, you've lost a lot of blood. I don't think you should stand just yet," Smee warned.

I instinctively tried to push myself upright, forgetting my current predicament, and immediately regretted my haste. Searing pain radiated through my mutilated limb the moment it touched the decking, quickly reminding me of the devastation inflicted by Pan. "Rum, now!" I gritted out through clenched teeth.

"Aye, Captain." Smee scurried off, leaving me with Kat and her pixie.

"Have the crew carry me to bed. I wish to be left alone."

I HAD POLISHED off an entire bottle of rum and was making a hefty dent in the second. It wasn't exactly great at masking the pain, but I'd been drinking it as though it were the cure to all my ails. A vain attempt to shut down my nagging thoughts. Nonetheless, they continued to cloud my mind.

Replaying the event over and over again in grueling, gruesome detail.

I couldn't make sense of why, when I had the chance, I fucking hesitated. I had him in my snares not once, but twice. Fucking twice! I was too concerned with *how* to kill him instead of just ending the feud once and for all. A simple death wasn't enough to suffice my demon. I had become greedy with revenge. And what boggled me the most, what ate at my very core, was Katherine. She had actually pleaded to save Pan's life. Whose side was she on? Could I trust her? Did she want to be their mother? I thought she loved me. I thought she was my other half. That we shared something special. But now, doubts plagued me.

The cabin door creaked open. "How are you doing?" Kat asked softly, peeking her head into the room. "May I come in?" She didn't wait for a response before making her way to my bedside. "I brought you something for the pain and some fresh bandages. We should clean the wound now that the bleeding has stopped. We don't want it to fester."

"I don't want your elixirs. What I need is more faerie dust. Where is that useless pixie of yours?"

"Meadow has already healed you as much as she can."

"Then where the fuck is my right hand, Katherine?" I lifted the useless stump so she could see it with her own eyes. "Why hasn't it grown back?"

Katherine's eyes welled with tears. "Meadow said there are things that can't be healed with faerie dust. I... I tried a few things while you were passed out. Nothing seems to be working. I'm tirelessly searching for a solution. But, like Meadow, my magic has limitations."

"The only thing limited here is your loyalty. Riddle me this, Miss Hawkins, did you know about the crocodile?" Rage began to boil in my heart. "You knew, and you said nothing."

"James, your eyes. They're red again."

"James, your eyes," I mocked. "I don't give a fuck about my damn eyes. Why didn't you warn me?"

"You know my visions are cryptic. I didn't know *this* was going to happen."

"What else are you keeping from me, huh? *You* are the reason I lost my hand, Katherine. *You* distracted my focus. *You* demanded that I spare the boy and leave Neverland behind."

"I was simp—"

"And why, pray tell, is my blood this god-forsaken color? Did you use magic on me, Miss Hawkins?"

"Meadow said it's from your deal with Tiger Lily. She used magic on you, not me. Or are you too drunk to remember your bargain with the Princess?"

"I'm sober enough to know *you*, the woman who claims to love me, can't be trusted. Where's Smee?"

Katherine took a deep breath. "He's with Starkey, managing the crew."

"Bring him to me. I'm done talking to you." She turned to leave, but I grabbed her arm. "Oh, and, Katherine, before you go, I believe you've taken something that belongs to me."

She looked at me quizzically. "I don't know—"

"Don't play coy with me. Give me back my ruby!"

Her brow furrowed, and her lips set in a hard line, but she remained silent as she fished the gemstone from her skirts. She threw it at me before turning on her heels and storming out the door.

Once I had the room to myself, I turned the ruby around in my fingers, watching how the facets bent the light to their whim. Not unlike the power the stone gifted to its steward. The consequences of using the Heart of the Divine weighed heavily on my mind. I'd only used it a handful of times, and now I couldn't help but wonder if the piper had come for his pound of flesh. I placed the ruby back safely in my pocket and made a silent vow to never abuse it again.

"Captain, Miss Hawkins said you were asking for me?" Smee poked his head into my cabin.

"Yes, please, come closer. Pull up a chair. We have much to discuss." I had to tell Smee about his son. He deserved closure, and I could at least offer him that much.

"It's a bleeding shame about your hand. How's the pain?"

"I've felt worse," I lied. I had never, in all my years of service to that masochist, Blackbeard, ever endured a pain even close to what I'd experienced at the hands of Pan.

Smee gave me a knowing smile but kept his thoughts to himself.

"Tell me, are my eyes red?" I stared at him, widening my eyes to ensure he got a good look.

"They look blue to me."

"That's what I thought." Katherine and Peter had been the only ones to ever mention it. They must have been seeing things. Either that or the two of them were conspiring against me. After what happened today, I couldn't be sure.

"Why do you ask?"

"No reason." I wasn't going to let Smee know of Katherine's attempt to drive me insane. I paused, frustrated, trying unsuccessfully to load my cigar holder with my only hand. I couldn't even smoke a goddamned cigar without fumbling.

Smee reached for the contraption. "Please, sir, let me help." He quickly placed the cigars and offered up a flame.

I inhaled deeply. Sweet relief. My irritable frustration quickly melted away as billows of white smoke curled from my nose. "You'd make a fine first mate. It's a shame I appointed you bo'sun."

"Thank you, Captain, but this is simply what friends do."

Friends, I hadn't had a *friend* since Henry. Losing him damn near killed me. The last thing I needed was another liability. I'd have to remember to keep the crew at a distance.

"I have news about Eli."

Smee's eyes lit up, and I instantly had his full attention.

I reached for his hand. "His remains are resting deep within the Viridianwood. I'm so sorry."

He pulled the glasses from his face and pinched the bridge of his nose. "How do you know this?"

"Pan confessed that Eli, along with others, are there."

Smee sat silently as a single tear slid down his cheek. "I

think I've known that Eli was gone for a while. I just never wanted to admit it to myself, and without proof, I had to keep searching for him."

"Take the crew on a search through the wood. Find your boy and give him a proper resting place."

"You need our help, Captain. I've waited this long for answers; I can wait a few more days. Waiting won't change the outcome."

"You'll do no such thing." I shook my head. "Go, find your son. I'll be here figuring out my next move. Oh, and Smee, if you happen to see that crocodile. I want her—alive. Bring her to me."

"Aye, Captain. I'll leave behind Starkey. He'll manage the ship while you recover. Thank you, James. I give you my word. When I return, we'll make things right. We *must* stop Peter Pan."

CHAPTER FIFTEEN
-VISIONS-
Katherine

He'd finally passed out in the captain's quarters, an empty bottle of rum still clutched in his only hand. Soiled bandages that seeped the strange aubergine blood were all that was left of his other. My hands trembled with exhaustion as I tidied up the room, leaving no evidence of the trauma that had occurred. James' soft snore disturbed the silence, and the monotonous tone grated on my frayed nerves. I'd tried everything to heal him, but I could never make him whole again, and that had broken him. I was a failure. I knew it. He knew it.

I'd watched him spiral into a darkness I wasn't sure he could come back from. He was so damn stubborn that he refused to let me give him the pain elixir, choosing rum instead, and it only made things worse. I resorted to slipping the potion into his bottle, along with a few herbs to make him sleep, unable to bear seeing him in any more pain.

I always knew James was plagued by demons. But I hadn't realized that he'd become one. The glaring red of his eyes still haunted me. He was no longer a mortal human. His strange blood confirmed that much to be true. He'd traded his soul away in the name of revenge. Where did that leave us?

THE SUN WAS SINKING into the sea by the time I gathered enough courage to leave the ship. "Let's go, Meadow. I can't stand it here another minute." She remained silent as I secured her tiny cage to my waist. The little pixie gave me quiet friendship when I needed it the most. No 'I told you so' or flippant comment. Only companionable silence, and I was ever grateful for it.

On the way out of our cabin, I stopped and hesitated at the table, warring with the idea of leaving him a note. I picked up the quill, ready to write a scathing goodbye. Words that had teeth enough to cut him. He deserved no less. But he'd been such a miserable prick to me that I couldn't bring myself to write anything. My silence would scream volumes.

I glanced at James one last time, finding him exactly

where I'd left him, eyes still closed in a drugged oblivion. I tried to swallow down the heartache as I thought of our earlier conversation. The way he had dismissed me so vehemently. He'd been more concerned about keeping that damned ruby than he was of me. I took a few tentative steps and knelt before him. Slipping my hand into his pocket, I pulled out the Heart of the Divine. I contemplated throwing it into the sea out of spite. The thought of his pain when he realized his precious ruby was gone forever brought a smile to my lips. But I couldn't let go of the possibility that the ruby could change our fate for the better, so without another thought, I quickly pocketed the gemstone. If James was too much of a coward to use it, maybe it was time to take fate into my own hands.

"Milady," Starkey called the moment I appeared on deck.

"Not now, Mr. Starkey. I'm in no mood for your questions. It's been a long day, and I need a moment to collect myself. I'll be back presently."

"Don't you think your place is here with him? He'll need you when he wakes," he pleaded with me, but James had proven that he didn't want me.

"He needs vengeance, Mr. Starkey. And I have no potions that can cure him of that." I shouldered past him without another word, focusing on my escape as the rocky shoreline of Neverland beckoned me. Melancholy had all but consumed me, and I needed to be alone with it. I checked one more time to ensure the ruby was safely tucked into the folds of my dress before leaving the *Jolly Roger* behind.

I walked for what felt like hours. Not talking. Simply existing. One foot in front of the other. One breath after the next. I don't remember seeing the landscape as it passed me by. I was becoming desperate to fix this rift between James and me. My mind began to drift to the ruby. Could I use it on James? Could I take away his memories of Peter and leave only memories of me? If that were even possible with whatever dark magic Tiger Lily had sewn into his soul. But if I could, would he still be the man I loved if I took that part of him away? My mind reeled with questions, and my heart ached all the more. There seemed to be no suitable answer.

The moon was nestled high in the sky when I finally collapsed. I found myself on the edge of a cliff. The Never Cliffs, as James had called them. I sat with my feet hanging over the edge peering down at the dizzying drop to the churning seas below.

It was the first time I allowed my surroundings to sink past the chaos in my mind. I could just make out the distant sound of drumming coming from the forest behind me. The faint flicker of lantern light filtered through the trees. It was a truly beautiful place teetering on the edge of Neverland. The ocean stretched out in an endless expanse before me as the stars peppered the sky.

"Do you know this place, Meadow?" They were the first words I'd spoken all night.

"Yes. The faerie camp is just beyond the trees," she chimed. Her own heavy-hearted voice made me wince. I pulled the tiny cage from my belt and held the little pixie to my face. Her tiny body glowed in a pale blue, belying her mood.

"I'm so sorry, my friend. If you can even call me that after I've kept you prisoner all this time."

"It's okay." She shrugged.

"It's not! I've kept you from your kin for far too long." I reached into the folds of my dress, fingering the ruby, and set my intentions. Who needed a key when I held the power of the cosmos in my hand? The tiny lock on the cage popped, and I opened the door, giving her the freedom she deserved. She perked up, her luminescence changing from a cool blue to a warm glow as she flitted out of the cage.

"Are you sure?"

"Right now, I'm more sure of this than anything else in my life."

"But won't you get into trouble if you let me go?"

"Now it's my turn to tell you it's okay. I need to start making decisions I can live with. You deserve to be free. James loves me, and that means he'll find a way to forgive me."

"You have a lot of faith in that bastard pirate of yours."

I chuckled at her, and it felt foreign. There had been little to laugh at lately and the realization of that brought a well of tears to my eyes. I'd been trying to live a fairytale life that had gotten so convoluted it more closely resembled a nightmare.

"Go on now. Go back to your home. I only hope that

you'll be able to forgive me, too," I choked out, trying to hold back the flood of tears.

"Good thing about pixies, we can only feel one emotion at a time. Makes it difficult to hold a grudge. But promise me something?" she asked, and I nodded, worried that if I spoke, I wouldn't be able to hold back the tears. "Don't hold on to the sadness for too long. Find a way to let it go and bring in a new emotion." She flitted up to my face, kissing my cheek briefly and, in a flurry of glitter, her little spark disappeared into the night sky.

I let the flood of tears fall. The only friend I had was gone. Leaving me alone with the broken pieces of my relationship with James, and I had no clue how to put them back together. My desperation morphed into anger.

"Why? Why does it have to be so hard?" I cried out to the night sky as I pounded my fists on the ground. I wasn't sure who I was talking to. But I wanted answers. I dug my fingers into the soil as the sobs raked over me, dirt and stone digging into my fingernails, scratching my skin. I clung to the life I'd envisioned for James and myself with everything I had, trying to find answers. Searching for the happily ever after that I so desperately wanted.

"It is because he is not your destiny," an ethereal voice echoed in my head. My heart cracked as the words took hold in my mind. It couldn't be true. James and I had a love that only ever happened once in a lifetime, if that.

A powerful vision slammed into my mind, causing me to

disassociate from my physical body. I found myself lying on the floor of a cottage. I scrambled to my feet, knowing the Divine was trying to show me something. I'd never had a vision of the future by simply touching the ground beneath me. Static white noise filled my ears. The scene was surreal. A peek through the veil of time into things that hadn't yet happened.

A large window looked out at the same view from the cliff tops where I'd collapsed. A dwelling had been built on the very spot at some point in the future. I turned from the window and sucked in a gasp. Behind me stood an enormous bed, and James sat on the edge, stroking the hair of a sleeping woman with beautiful chestnut hair fanning out around her. There was a look of adoration in James' eyes as he stared at her.

He got up from the bed and approached me.

"James?" I whispered, feeling as though I was intruding on a private moment. But his gaze never met mine. A shiver passed through me as his body ghosted through mine. Nausea welled in my stomach as I turned to him. He stood at the window, looking out over the sea. A polished hook, where his hand should be, glinted in the early morning light. He was older here, his skin bronzed by the sun, and the lines of his face seemed sharper. He had that graceful elegance of maturity, along with a litany of new scars and tattoos across his chest. But for all the time that now etched his face, the deep lines of torment that had cut across his brow, the ones I was so used to seeing, were gone. He stroked his beard, a smile gracing his lips. He was happy. I could feel it radiating off him.

"No, James. This isn't real. I am here!" I turned to the specter of James, pleading with him to see me. To hear me. Instead, he turned to look at the woman in the bed, his smile growing as he gazed at her. I reached for him, trying to turn his face to mine, but my hand moved through him, and the vision disappeared. I was alone on the cliffs again.

I rubbed at my tear-streaked eyes, wondering if I'd gone mad. It wasn't like any other vision I'd had before. I wanted to deny the truth of it. But it had been so real. And if I were honest with myself, I knew that I'd seen James' future. One that didn't include me.

I'd never felt so alone. My entire life's purpose, all the plans I had for the future poured through my hands like shifting sands. The churning waves of the sea below beckoned me forward. I couldn't stand to watch as another took my place at James' side. One more step took me to the edge, my toes hugging the lip of the rock. I spread my arms and let the breeze whip around me. Maybe the sea would welcome me into her watery embrace. Maybe there I'd find the peace I was searching for.

"I wouldn't be doing that if I were you, sweetness." A gravelly voice cut through the calm of the breeze. I must have died because that voice truly belonged on the other side.

"Edward?" I asked, whirling to see the dark, imposing

figure of Edward Teach. "How am I here? I don't even remember jumping."

"Oh, I'm here alright. Alive and in the flesh."

"Are we not dead? I know you're dead. I saw your body."

A dark chuckle escaped his lips, and I knew then that Edward had somehow remained in the land of the living. He took another step toward me, but I had nowhere to go. It was Teach or the watery grave below. My heart thundered in my chest while my mind tried to play catch up to the quickly shifting circumstances.

"James was sorely mistaken if he thought your weak little poison would finish me off," he boasted. "You stopped him from slitting my throat. That's when I knew you still had some love for me, after all. He never should have listened to you."

"That wasn't love, it was mercy," I argued.

His hand shot out and grabbed my neck, dragging me from the cliff and slamming me against his chest.

"Don't you touch me," I managed as his hand squeezed my throat, and I tried, in vain, to push him away. I stilled when I felt his blade at my bodice. The thin fabric was all that kept me from the unforgiving point.

"Listen to me, pet. I'm not here for revenge. Only James holds fast to such naïve notions. I'm here to arrange a deal. A new contract between you and me."

"I'm not your property anymore. I'll die before I let that happen again."

"I can't force you into anything. But once you see the

changes I'm prepared to make, your pussy will be dripping with the thought of being mine."

"I'm with James." I tried to sound indignant, but the vision I'd just seen had cast a shadow of doubt over me. And the gleam in Edward's eyes told me he saw it, too.

He chuckled. "You don't think I know my wayward bo'sun? His heart only has room for vengeance. Aren't you tired of playing second fiddle to his vendetta?"

A lump formed in my throat. The truth of his words gutted me. "You're one to talk. I was always second to your quest for the ruby."

"I'm not denying that. But you've got the ruby now, don't you?"

"I don't know what you're talking about," I said, lifting my chin in my best effort to convince him of my bluff.

"Don't lie to me! I can feel the power radiating off you."

I pulled the ruby from my pocket and thrust my hand out over the cliff. "I'll drop it," I challenged.

"You won't drop it. You know how important it is. I know you're searching for answers. For once in your life, you're questioning your visions."

"You can't know that."

"For a woman who can see the future, the only reason you'd choose to end this life is if you saw something you couldn't live with. But there may be another way. Let me help you, and then you can decide which path to follow."

CHAPTER SIXTEEN
-DEBTS-
Katherine

"Where are you taking me?" I asked, failing miserably to keep the irritation out of my voice.

"To see an old friend," Edward said. He'd been suspiciously quiet as he led me deeper inland. Luring me to follow him with promises that he could give me answers. And yet he remained annoyingly silent. I was beginning to wonder if I'd made a mistake. I hadn't been in my right mind, and the initial shock of his resurrection from the dead compelled me to follow. But the longer I followed him, the more my rational brain questioned the choices I was making.

Edward was relentless, pushing on through the night, the two of us absconding in the darkness. The monotony of pace and Edward's perpetual silence had my mind wandering to James. What would happen when he slept off the rum? What would he do when he realized I was gone? The vindictive side of me hoped my absence would crush him. Bring him to the realization that he'd truly fucked up. I wanted him to feel the same pain that had taken up permanent residence in my heart.

But the other half of me worried. Would he be in pain? Who would tend his bandages? Had he spiked a fever during the night? If my vision was to be believed, James still had a long life ahead of him, regardless of his injury. Which brought on a new layer of anxiety that pooled in my belly. What if that life no longer included me?

When the white tower of the Temple Mount rose from the canopy, it was clear what our destination was. Meadow had piqued my interest when she mentioned the place. Apparently, Edward was also aware of the great knowledge and power the temple possessed. The idea that someone here might be able to help me decipher my visions allowed a small kernel of hope to bloom in my chest. I was desperate to find a reason, any reason at all, that my vision had been wrong.

We passed through an arched entrance into the main courtyard. Though we were cloaked by a dense mist in the shadowed dawn, there was no need to hide. The Temple was open. No doors or guards were there to deter us. Ivory walls seemed to glow in the waning moonlight, and the grounds hummed with a primitive power. The very building funneled energy around it like a conduit.

"You have friends here?" I asked, remembering that this was a place of worship. A notion that was completely at odds with the man I knew.

"I have friends everywhere."

"Why do I think you're using the term 'friend' loosely?"

He turned to glare at me. "The man you see before you today is a product of circumstance. I wasn't always this way."

"Man? Don't you mean *fae*?" Edward's glare turned deadly, and I swallowed hard, knowing I was testing his patience. He turned his back on me, ending the conversation. It was an obvious dismissal and further indication that he wasn't interested in discussion. The honesty of his statement began to sink in. I realized that I, too, was a different person now. Forever altered after all I'd been through. As we marched on, I mourned silently for the woman I once was because she was surely dead now.

He led me down a hallway of doors, stopping at the last one in the row. I jumped at the sound of his fist pounding on the heavy wooden slab, rattling it on its hinges. When no one answered, he knocked again, harder this time.

"Maybe your friend doesn't live here anymore," I suggested, but he ignored me.

"Come on, Amara. Open up. I know you're in there!" he commanded and continued to pound on the door.

"Edward! We're making a scene. I think—"

"What's so important that it cannot wait until morning?" A distinctly feminine voice called out before the door opened a crack. "Éadbard? My Divine, is it really you?" she said with a condescending smile.

The door opened a fraction more, revealing a beautiful nymph cast in the glow of candlelight from within. Her features were stately and distinguished. High cheekbones and a finely chiseled nose gave her an heir of superiority. Dark curls cascaded over a blanket that was pulled tight around her shoulders, a hint of gray woven through the strands.

"Cut the pretense, Amara. I know you're not delighted to see me."

"What are you doing here?" she hissed as she stuck her neck out and scanned the hallway, her eyes fixating on me.

"I need to see him. I have a favor to collect," he said, drawing her intrusive stare from me.

"I don't know who you're talking about."

"Don't play dumb with me. You've been sneaking him into your private quarters for centuries now. Some things never change."

She stared at him, her mouth set in a sharp line of contemplation before she waved us into her room, scanning the hallways once more before closing the door behind us.

"You are in exile and distinctly male. It would be improper for you to be seen entering the private quarters of a priestess at night," she scolded.

"Don't act like you're a stickler for the rules. I'm sure your cunning mind could come up with an excuse if we get caught."

"You can come out, Kían," she called to the seemingly empty room.

A half-dressed male stumbled from behind a curtain, pulling his pants into place. The middle-aged fae straightened himself and promptly rubbed his eyes in disbelief.

"Kían! Friend, time has been good to you, I see," Edward said warmly.

"Wish I could say the same for you," Kían sneered, giving Edward a not-so-warm welcome. "What are you doing here? *How* are you even here?"

"I'm delighted to see you as well," Edward said, evading his question with overtly sarcastic formality.

"You show up uninvited and unannounced at the crack of dawn, and you expect us to welcome an exiled fae into our home with open arms? With a strange mortal on your arm, no less. Who the hell is she, anyway?"

"This is Katherine. Soon to be my mate." The pair looked at me, their eyes widening as they took me in. I'm sure a similar expression was plastered on my face, but it wasn't the time or place to argue with him.

"A human woman?" Kían asked.

"Not just any human. She's one of the few in the thirteenth realm that's been blessed with the early seeds of magic."

"Hmm, poor girl," he said, his appraisal of me turning to pitiful disgust. Amara, however, had a flash of curiosity cross her gaze before she covered it with a mask of indifference.

"Edward," I whispered, pulling at his sleeve to get his attention. "What are we doing here? I think we should go."

"Nonsense. You wanted answers, right? And now I'm in the market to collect on that favor I am owed."

"I'm not throwing you out on your ass in respect for the friendship we once had," Kían started. "But you know the laws of the realms. You're in exile. If I help you and they find out—"

"Are you enjoying this fine life here in Neverland?" Edward interrupted. "What was the name of that position I secured for you?" Edward stroked his beard, an amused look on his face. A look I was all too familiar with. He was playing with his prey. "Oh yes, Magister! I'm sure that being a scholar of such high order offers you many luxuries and great status among the people here. It would be a shame for me to undo all that I have done for you."

"Éadbard, it's not that simple—"

"It is that simple. Katherine," Edward said, reaching a hand to me. "Give me the stone." I felt all the eyes in the room fall on me. I knew that if I didn't produce the ruby, Edward would easily rip it from my body once he'd punished me for disobeying him. This was a mistake, and it was all my fault. I fished it from my pocket and set a world of power in his outstretched palm. "It's all so simple because I have the

Heart of the Divine." The presence of the ruby was all it took to silence the room.

<small>EARLY MORNING RAYS</small> filtered into the Temple Mount's immense library, illuminating a pile of dusty books. I blinked back the fatigue that made my head ache. I'd been awake for far too long, and the strain of it all was wearing me thin.

"It might help if you tell us what exactly you're looking for," Amara grumbled as she closed yet another ancient tome.

"Amara, you disappoint me. I thought, of all people, you would've had me all figured out. All these books are nothing more than historical accounts."

"We may learn something in the histories. Maybe someone discovered a loophole to the ruby's power," I said, trying to be useful even though I had no idea what we were looking for. I'd been led to believe that Edward brought me here to help with my visions. But it was clear he had ulterior motives, and he'd kept me completely in the dark about them.

Edward's cold eyes shifted to me. A condescending smile on his face. "You look a lot prettier with your mouth closed."

My jaw clenched as I held my tongue. Not a single day had passed, and he'd fallen back into his old ways. I was still nothing more than property to him. His obsession with the ruby hadn't changed. I was the fool for believing he could be any different. Each passing moment confirmed that I had made a mistake following Edward. But even if I wanted to leave and give up my chance at finding answers, Edward wouldn't oblige.

"Amara, I don't need detailed notes on how the Heart of the Divine came into being. I need something that dares to be more," Edward said.

"Don't expect me to read your mind! One cannot predict the actions of a fae who's truly lost his soul," Amara snapped.

Edward chuckled as he leaned back in his chair. "It's because you have no vision, Amara. You're trapped inside a little box the Divine has put you in. I'm ready to break the chains."

"Be plain, Éadbard! I'm growing weary of your riddles. You came to collect a favor, but you have yet to name that favor. What do you want?" Kían asked, slamming a fist on the table.

"You ruin all the fun, Kían. There is a particular text that contains rituals, ones the Divine never wanted us to know. *The Book of Divine Desecration.*"

"That book no longer exists. All the copies were destroyed ages ago, and for good reason," Amara said dismissively.

"Is that so? You see, I have it on good authority that not all of them were destroyed. Twelve copies were spared. One sent to each of the magic-wielding realms for safekeeping." Amara remained silent, and it was as much of an admission as if she'd come right out and said it. "Once you bring me that book, I'll acquire the same unfettered power as the

Divine. The book outlines a ritual that will extract the ruby's power from its corporeal restraints, releasing it from Divine rules that deny us true power," he said as he examined the seemingly insignificant ruby that he rolled in his fingers. "Now, be a good little priestess and fetch the book for me."

"In another lifetime, we may have been friends, but until you tell us what you're planning to do with this power once you've obtained it, we don't go any further," Kían said, taking an offensive stand in front of his mate.

Edward crossed his arms over his chest, a sinister smirk crossing his face. "As I see it, you have one of two options. You tell her to get me the book I need, and once I become the most powerful fae in history, I will bestow endless gifts on those who help me. Or... we can sit here and argue the finer points of morality. But beware, the longer you take, the more likely the bastard prince will soon discover my whereabouts. Now that I've returned to the fae realms, I cannot elude his magic. I may be mistaken, but I would suspect that you'd rather not call that kind of attention to your little piece of paradise. Go ahead. Take all the time you need. We all know that in the end, I'll get what I want."

My skin crawled at the vision of evil that had chased us out of Mag Mel. Amara's eyes widened at the mere mention of his name. His reputation obviously preceded him.

"Amara, go and fetch him the book he is looking for," Kían said stoically.

She stared at her mate, and a look of disgust creased her face. "You're a fucking coward," she said to him as she pushed up from the table. "You," she pointed at me, "come with me. You're my assurance that Kían will remain unharmed until we return."

I followed close behind the priestess. Her petite form moving with speed and purpose, leading me to the lower levels of the library. The temperature dropped as we descended, and the dank smell of stagnant air grew stronger. Amara pressed her hand against a plate at each door we encountered in order to gain entrance. I had a feeling that I would never make it out of here alive if she decided to leave me behind.

"What have you gotten yourself into, girl?" she asked, shaking her head. And I knew that this might be my only opportunity to get the answers I needed. I could see through Edward's deception. He'd never meant to help me with my visions. I was, and always had been, a pawn in his plan.

"I was told you could help me. You're a priestess, right? Does that mean you have powers?"

She looked back at me with a raised eyebrow. "What does a human woman know of the Divine's gifts?" she said as she entered through yet another door and led us into a small void of a room. She lifted her hand, and a glowing orb of light manifested over her outstretched palm. A clear testament that she did indeed possess magic. I followed her into a circular room, my eyes fixated on the orb of light. Once inside, the door behind us closed of its own accord, the impact stirring the dust from the shelves.

"Who are you?" she demanded.

"I'm no one. I'm just an insignificant human."

"You're not just a human. I wasn't expecting it so soon, but could you be—" She hesitated for a moment and then reached for me. I let her curl her cool hands over my wrists.

Her touch hit me like a tempest, an otherworldly power slamming into me. This wasn't like any vision I'd ever had. It was as if I was being split in two. As I pulled the future from her, she tore it from me with equal ferocity. It was a jumbled exchange, a whirlwind of overwhelming feelings I couldn't piece together. Until a vision became crisp in my mind.

A forked path in the woods.

To the left, James stood alone. A hook, where his hand had been, glinted in the sunlight.

To the right was darkness. And there I crouched, keening over James' lifeless body.

The vision erupted in smoke, and I saw her, the priestess, flickering in my consciousness as my power overturned hers, and a new vision appeared.

A field.

A growing storm.

Power and death.

A sacrifice.

A brunette girl—*that girl!*

Amara ripped her hands away from me, and we both doubled over as though we'd been struck. I stumbled away from her on shaky legs, desperately trying to catch my breath.

"What did you do to me?" I managed to get out.

"Me? You are not at all what you seem. You may not be the one I've been waiting for, but the Divine surely has a plan for you."

"Who is she? I've seen that girl before. Who is she?" I demanded, desperate for more answers.

"She is a chosen, just like you. We all have our path. Now listen carefully, we don't have much time. The Divine has made it all so clear." She turned to the shelves and busied herself, looking through the books, a sense of urgency filling the small room.

"I've had a vision of James with that girl. But that cannot be his future. *I am* his future, not her. That's why I came to you. I need answers."

"Not all of us were fated for such a beautiful life. Some of us have a higher purpose."

"No, it can't be. For all the things that have happened to me, he is what made it all worth it. James is *my* gift." My voice cracked as the emotions welled up inside me.

"I'm sorry, my child, but this was not meant to last forever. You've surely witnessed the signs? The very universe is conspiring to end one path and start you down the next. Be honest with yourself. You may love him, but you've already begun to see the fatal flaws in that love, haven't you?"

The tears were flowing freely now as the truth became too clear to deny any longer. I sunk to my knees as the sobs turned into wails. The only protest I had was against an ending that I could not change. My heart was breaking, and there was nothing to do but allow the darkness to consume me.

"Katherine!" Amara said, wrapping her firm hands around my arms and pulling me to my feet. I heard the crack before I felt the sting of her hand against my cheek. The slap cut through the anguish that was drowning me. "Pull yourself together. You have a purpose. It may not be the way you envisioned it, but your life has meaning."

"I don't know if I can do it. I don't think I can go on without him." My chin trembled with the agony of it all and the fear of this unknown future I'd have to face alone.

"The female line is ever enduring. Even in our darkest hour, we find a way to go on, to do what we must. To persevere. Find solace in your resilience." I couldn't speak. I could only nod, even though I wasn't sure I'd survive this. "Now listen to me carefully. I cannot stop Éadbard from releasing the power of the ruby from its bonds. The Divine meticulously shaped the gemstone, embedding it with their power. Crafting it for the specific purpose of governing the magic within. These sacred rules are what maintain the delicate balance. If he should control such raw power with no constraints, it would spell out the demise of all the realms." She stared at me intently, giving me a moment to let her words sink in. "I cannot stop him from siphoning off the power, but he needs me to perform the ritual. I can alter it to bind the power to someone else. I can tie the magic to a mortal soul. One that will keep it safe."

"What? I don't understand what you're asking."

"I'm telling you that you've been chosen to be the bearer of this power. To keep it safe from those who would abuse it."

"But that's not possible. It's in the rules. The Heart of the Divine cannot be bound to any one person," I countered, desperate for any way out of this.

"When the power contained in the ruby is released, the rules binding it will be broken. That is why it is so dangerous. It will have the ability to upend destinies. It must be protected. Do you understand?"

"Why can't I be this guardian you need and still be with James? With that power, I could take away all the pain from this vendetta with Pan. We could live a happy life away from all of this."

"It is not so. James and Peter are tightly woven into the fabric of fate. Their story must play out. Our very existence depends on it. It is no simple task the Divine has given you. You will be hunted for the power you possess. You must take it and go into hiding."

"James will never let me leave. He loves me just as much as I love him. If our roles were reversed, I would never accept it," I said defiantly, reaching for any way to unravel these chains that were constricting around me.

"You must make it happen. James has a role to play here in Neverland. His heartbreak is part of the story, a piece of the puzzle. You have seen what will happen to him if you choose the wrong path."

I'd never felt so completely out of control in my entire

life. A life that wasn't even mine anymore. I could feel my love, my humanity, drain out of me, leaving nothing but an empty husk behind. Once, I'd thought that the worst thing that could happen to me was to be Edward's property, but now I was a pawn in a much bigger game. My only salvation was to allow my heart to shrivel and die. It was devastatingly poetic. I would hold the power of the universe at my fingertips, yet I'd be completely powerless.

CHAPTER SEVENTEEN
-WARRANTED-
James

I rubbed at my dry, gritty eyes, squinting to block out the day's light shining into my cabin like a torturous beam of agony. The blasted sun had shown its face yet again. Pain throbbed in my head like a hammer, pounding at my brow. What time was it? Fuck, what day was it? I'd consumed enough rum to kill a small horse, and yet here I was. Alive and paying the price for my overindulgence.

Images of Pan's sinister smile as he dropped my hand to the crocodile hissing below flashed in my mind. I looked down at my right arm, still wrapped in blood-stained bandages. Blood that was no longer crimson but a strange, aubergine color. The memories weren't simply a nightmare. It had happened, and it was time to face my truth. Hesitating, I fingered the edges of the fabric. I would never again be the man I once was. I had changed both physically and mentally.

Peter himself had sealed my fate, tossing my severed hand into the jaws of the crocodile. How was it that he, a mere boy, was the single cause of all my pain and suffering? It was as though he was put here to punish me for all my previous lives' sins. All I *ever* did was grow up. I had no choice in the matter. And look at me now. Pathetic. I wiped away the traitorous tear sliding down my cheek and decided, then and there, I was done feeling sorry for myself. I was Captain James of the *Jolly Roger*. I was going to offer refuge to the innocent Lost Boys Peter cast out. I was going to make a difference. It was my destiny to end Peter fucking Pan at any cost. Taking a deep breath, I pulled off the bandages, forcing myself to look at what was left of my arm.

It was gruesome. My already sour stomach turned, causing me to retch at the mere sight of it. It was still quite tender to the touch, although considerably better than yesterday. The bleeding had more or less stopped. Nothing but a few oozing spots and some black-crusted scabs forming over a mottled stump. New skin had just started to form over the raw tissue. Still semi-translucent in its infancy. I could see the bone and arteries mending just under the surface. Magic was definitely at play here. Without the interference of Katherine and her pixie, I'd surely be dead. And though they had tried, there was no hope of my hand growing back. A detail I struggled to accept. I was permanently disfigured.

Learning to use my left hand was going to prove challenging. I did everything with my right, eating, writing, fighting, taking a piss, pleasuring Katherine. Speaking of Kat, I wondered where she was? She hadn't been in to see me yet today. At least not since I had woken. I'd been cruel to her in my drunken delirium. My enchanted tattoo assured that I remembered every single regrettable word. I needed to find her and make amends.

"STARKEY!" I'd made my way to the quarterdeck, holding up my breeches with my one hand. I couldn't even dress myself without help. Where was everyone? "Starkey!"

"Captain!" Starkey came running from the main deck. "You're up… and about? I wasn't expecting—"

"Tie my damn breeches."

"Uhh," Starkey looked at my waist, befuddled. "Oh, you can't—" He stopped short. "Aye, Captain."

"What day is it?"

"Tis the day after yesterday, sir."

I looked at him blankly and sighed at his stupidity. "How long have I been asleep?"

"Oh, forgive me, Captain. It's midday. You slept through morning."

I sighed again, still not getting the answer I was looking for. "Where is Miss Hawkins? I haven't yet seen her today."

Starkey stared at me, his eyes widening, his face going pale.

"Where. Is. Miss. Hawkins?" I said the words comically slow this time. Clearly, I misjudged Starkey's ability to carry the position of first mate.

"I...sir, I..."

"Out with it!"

"She left with the pixie last night. She has not yet returned."

"What do you mean she left?" Katherine wasn't a prisoner. She could come and go at her will. But she never returned? That was cause for concern.

"I tried to stop her. She—"

"Where is Smee?"

"You sent him off with the rest of the crew. To find his son."

"Ah, yes. I remember. So, *no one* has gone looking for her?"

"No, Captain."

"You imbecile! Do you have any idea of the danger she could be in? If one hair on her perfect head is harmed, you will find yourself moldering in the Viridianwood."

"I... I—"

"Get my cutlass. Now!"

"Yes, Captain." Starkey scurried off, returning promptly with my sword.

"Move my scabbard to the right side of my belt. I'm going in search of Miss Hawkins."

"Sir, respectfully, you can't."

"Last time I checked, I was the captain of this ship. You'd be wise to remember that. Send Smee out to find me upon his return. I won't be back until I've found her."

WHAT WAS SHE THINKING? She knew better than to go off on her own in the middle of the night. Surely, she wouldn't have gone into the Viridianwood? I'd warned her of the dangers there. That pixie of hers would have guided her elsewhere, right? Fuck! Katherine, where did you go? Neverland was a small island. She couldn't be far. Maybe she'd gone to Tiger Lily looking for a way to mend my hand. Yes! That's it. I'll start there.

The alternative option was unthinkable. Could she have really betrayed me and run off to be the surrogate mother to Peter and his Lost Boys? The idea sent a vicious chill down my spine. There was no way she'd turncoat. Not Katherine. We'd been through too much together. We loved each other. She was soft, sure. Her maternal side wouldn't allow her to see past the 'young boy' Peter appeared to be. I'd explained to her he was hundreds if not thousands of years old, but it didn't help. I couldn't fault her for that. It was a boggling thing to comprehend. It went against nature. I pushed the intrusive thoughts from my mind and continued north to Tiger Lily's village. That's where I would find her. My beloved was searching for a solution to my situation.

"TIGER LILY!" I roared, walking straight into the village center. "Show yourself, or I'll end this satyr's life right now." I'd grabbed a young male on the outskirts of the village and had my cutlass digging into his throat. It was a ballsy move. If any of Tiger Lily's guards came at me, I'd be a dead man. With my dominant hand gone, I was essentially defenseless. But I wanted answers, and I wanted them now. The village had been quiet, but my outburst had drawn attention, and a crowd was forming quickly.

"Jas, old friend." Tiger Lily emerged from her home, confusion quickly contorting her beautiful face. "This is not how you get my attention."

"It's not? Huh? It appears to be working exactly how I had planned."

"Release the boy."

"I want answers first. Katherine, is she with you?"

"Katherine? Why would she be with me?"

"I had a run-in with Pan, and I believe she may have come to you for help."

"I've not seen your mistress nor heard of this 'run-in.'"

I waved my stump for Tiger Lily to see as the gathering crowd gasped around me. "The bastard has disfigured me."

"Clearly, you must have done *something* to deserve this punishment. The Divine does not just take away without warrant."

"I have no desire to discuss the logistics. Pan will get what's coming for him. I'd advise you to stay out of the way or find yourself with the same fate." I took a step closer, keeping the young satyr under my blade. "Why is my blood now a vile shade of purple?"

"You came to me seeking blood magic. What did you expect would happen? Were you so naïve to believe you wouldn't be changed?"

"What kind of demon have you turned me into?"

"I never changed you into a demon. That piece of you was already there. The magic simply altered your blood. This cannot be undone."

"You didn't tell me there would be consequences for my request."

"Oh, I did. You chose not to hear it. Tell me, James, are you now ungrateful for your memories?"

"Where is Katherine?" I asked again. Ignoring her remarks. "Someone must have seen her. If you're hiding her from me, this boy will be the least of your worries."

"We have not seen your missing woman. Release the boy and leave my village before I have my guard remove you."

Frustrated, I spun around the young satyr, slicing my cutlass through the air and lobbing off his small hand in one fell swoop. An eye for an eye, right? The surrounding crowd screamed in sync with the boy, rushing to his side. A pool of bright red blood blooming at his cloven feet. I turned and simply walked away from the growing chaos. "Ask your *Divine* what he did to deserve *that*. I'm sure it was warranted."

THE DAY QUICKLY GREW LATE, and there was still no sign of Kat anywhere. I'd searched the Mermaid Lagoon and even bloodied the waters with one of their own after she made a vile comment about Katherine and how I'd be better off without her. For such beautiful creatures, they were ugly on the inside. I ensured that they would think before they spoke in the future.

Kat wasn't hiding in the grotto either. I was running out of places to look. Desperation began to gnaw at my breaking heart. I refused to believe that she had run off with Peter. She would never hurt me like that. We had plans for a future together. Had I said something I didn't remember last night? The enchantment wouldn't allow that. Or was I so far gone that I—

"Captain?" A disembodied male voice called out through the trees, startling me. I scanned the surroundings, my bloodied cutlass poised and ready.

"Captain James? Is that you?" Smee popped out from behind a large tree, sending me whirling.

"Smee, for fuck's sake! Where did you come from?"

"Starkey sent me looking for ya. He said you were out searching for Miss Hawkins."

"Yes! Was she back on the ship?"

"No, Captain."

I sighed, completely defeated. This was not the news I'd been hoping for. "I was beginning to think I hadn't yet found her simply because she had gone back home. Did she say anything to you last night before she left?"

"No, but in all fairness, I was on a mission to find my son. I didn't exactly linger after our conversation."

"Were you able to find Eli?"

Smee adjusted his spectacles. "Aye, I believe it was him we found in the Viridianwood." His chin quivered, and he wiped at his cheek, sweeping away a fallen tear. "We brought him and three others to the edge of the tree lines, looking out at Three Pence Bay, and gave them a proper burial. Pan must be stopped before he kills another innocent."

"You have my word. I will not stop until Pan is dead and molding with the fallen leaves. The beasts will feast upon his rotting flesh, and through their *shit*, he will become the very island that worships him."

Smee smiled, delight sparkling in his eyes as he pulled me in for a hug. "I pledge to you my undying loyalty. Together, we will stop him, my friend."

There was that word again, friend. I needed to shift the dynamic. I appreciated Smee's fealty and admired his devotion, but I could not, would not, allow him into my heart. I've experienced enough pain to last several lifetimes. The last thing I wanted was another person to care about.

"Smee, old man, I need to piss. Help me with my breeches." If holding up my pants while I pissed didn't show Smee his place, I don't know what would.

"Do you need me to hold your cock, too?"

"No!" I gruffed, grabbing my dick before he could put his hands on it. "Just hold up my damn breeches and tie me back up after."

"Were you right-handed?" he asked, making small talk while I relieved myself.

"Aye."

"I guess you're going to have to relearn how to do the most basic things. How are you—"

"I don't know, Smee. I fucking jerk off with my right hand, too. Did you want to offer me a hand with that as well?"

Smee chuckled, "I'm sorry. I can't imagine what you're going through. If there is anything I can do to help, I'm at your service."

"Can you grow my hand back?" I paused, waiting for an answer that wouldn't come. "No? I didn't think so. There is nothing that can be done. I'm half a man."

"Hands do not make you a man, James. It's your power, your strength, your prick. As I just witnessed, that piece of you is still very much intact. Stop feeling sorry for yourself. Your injury can either define you or make you stronger. A man understands that you can lose a battle but still win the war. The choice is yours."

I huffed as he tied my breeches. I didn't need the pep talk from Smee. He had no idea what it was like to lose a literal piece of yourself at the hands of your nemesis. He may have lost a son, but at least his body was still in one piece. I just wanted to find Katherine and put an end to this day. "I'm *choosing* to go back to the *Jolly Roger*. Surely, Katherine has returned home by now."

THE SUN HAD BEGUN its nightly descent when we arrived back at the ship. Pink and peach hues painted the sky in a beautiful blush. The crew scurried about the deck as if nothing were amiss. I took a moment and said a silent plea to the Divine. Please let my Katherine be home, and in one piece.

"Starkey!"

He was startled at the sound of my voice. "Captain, you're back."

"Aye. Where is Miss Hawkins?"

The smile dropped from his face. "She's not with you, sir?"

"Fuck!" My stomach dropped. "I thought maybe she had come home."

"Smee!" Cecco interrupted, breathless from running

across the deck with a box in hand. "A package was delivered while you were gone. It's from Rindle, the gnome. He said it was most important."

"Oh! Yes, I wasn't expecting them to get it here so fast. Well, no better time than now." Smee grabbed the box and turned to me.

"Captain, I hope I'm not overstepping my boundaries but, I wanted to thank you for helping me find my son. And for giving these cast-off Lost Boys a family. *This* is for you." He knelt before me and offered up the wooden box.

Carved across the top in the most beautiful script were the words Captain James Hook. Puzzled, I looked at Smee.

"Open it, Captain."

I slowly lifted the lid. Curiosity filled my stomach with nervous excitement. Nestled upon a bed of crimson velvet lay a polished silver hook attached to an ornately decorated cuff. I had never seen anything like it before. It was beautiful. I stared, speechless, tracing a finger along the cool metal curve. The tip had been sharpened into a wicked point, pricking my skin as I explored. "Smee, it's… exquisite."

"The gnomes assured me it would fit. Why don't you slide it on and see how it feels?"

The weight seemed impeccably balanced as I held it in my hand. I slid my healing stump painfully into the cuff and watched in disbelief as the intricately embossed filigree danced across the metal, forming the base to my severed wrist.

"Well? How does it feel?" Smee asked hesitantly.

"It's perfect." A cool breeze at the back of my neck sent a shiver down my spine, and I smiled, knowing everything was about to change. A sinister laugh bellowed from my chest. The crew stood motionless and wide-eyed at my new addition. "From this moment forward, I am to be known as Captain James Hook."

Smee stood smiling, raising my arm and my new hook to the sky. "All hail Captain Hook!"

"Cap-tain Hook! Cap-tain Hook!" The crew chanted, lifting me high into the air, celebrating my new nom de guerre.

The boisterous excitement had blissfully pulled my attention from Katherine's whereabouts. It was the first time since the incident that I'd had a moment of real happiness. Thanks to Smee and his brilliant token of appreciation, the future was looking much brighter.

"Rum for everyone! We have much to celebrate."

The air around us thickened. Something was amiss. I felt the atmospheric shift in my bones. The scent of ozone was heavy in the air. The crew fell silent, and I looked at Smee, silently beckoning him to me, when what looked like a burst of smoke and glittering gunpowder exploded mere feet in front of me.

My heart stopped dead in my chest. I couldn't believe my eyes. I had to be hallucinating. There, standing in front of me as the smoke dissipated, was my beloved Katherine and beside her slight frame was a familiar face from my nightmares—Blackbeard.

CHAPTER EIGHTEEN
-FORSAKEN-
James

"You!" I growled. The initial relief of seeing Katherine safe and unharmed was immediately replaced with a burning rage at seeing my old mentor seemingly well and resurrected from the dead.

"Ahh, James, you look surprised to see me." He let out a sinister chuckle.

"Katherine, are you alright?" I asked, my eyes never leaving Teach. She looked unharmed, but Teach was good at hiding abuse, and not all wounds left physical marks. I needed reassurance she was well. "Are you hurt? Did this fucker hurt you?" My hand shifted to my cutlass, ready to gut the man if he'd harmed one hair on her head.

"I'm fine, James." Her voice sounded despondent, sending a chill down my spine. Even her eyes looked vacant, staring right through me as I took a step toward her.

"What have you done to her?"

"I see balance has been restored, and you've finally paid the price for your disloyalty," he started, dismissing my question as he gestured to the newly fitted hook. This derailed me from my chivalrous defense of Katherine and sent my mind reeling at the implications of his words. Was *he* the reason the Divine had taken my hand? Had this been the reason Tiger Lily had alluded to? I'd sworn fealty to him years ago, even allowed him to leave his brand on my skin. But my loyalty had withered and died as my love for Katherine grew. I hurried to mask my thoughts. There would be time for contemplation later. Now, I couldn't afford to show this man any weakness.

"I'm growing rather fond of it," I said, admiring the polished steel. "I consider it an upgrade. And it makes for a fetching moniker—Captain James Hook. Has a nice ring to it, don't you think?"

"Says the mortal, who's now only half a man."

"You really are slipping in your old age," I tsked as I rolled up my sleeves, ensuring he got a good glimpse of the tattoo that now covered his brand. "If you truly knew your enemy, you'd have known that I severed the ties of fealty to you long ago. I am far from being the mortal man you remember." I settled the sharp point of the hook on my forearm, pausing for dramatic effect before dragging it across my skin, giving the steel its first taste of blood. A flicker of fear flashed across Blackbeard's face as the warm trickle of aubergine blood ran down my arm.

"It doesn't matter what blood magic you sold your soul for. I already own it. You can cover my brand all you want, but until I'm dead, your soul belongs to me. It's over for you, *Hook*," he hissed. "Honestly, you should let me end it now. It would be mercy. You're a washed-up has-been. You can't even defeat a young boy. And now... now your woman is about to leave your prick in the dirt."

That was all I needed to push me over the edge. Edward and I had to settle this once and for all. The demon roared in my chest. I couldn't see it for myself, but I knew my eyes glowed red. A manifestation of the burning hatred that consumed me.

I charged at him, a feral battle cry ripping from my lungs. I put my entire weight into the swing, using the momentum to land a devastating blow. It was impressive, even for my left hand. Immense pain radiated all the way to my shoulder, but it was worth it to watch Edward stumble across the deck, barely keeping himself upright. It took a moment for him to straighten himself. Saliva and thick, purple blood poured from his mouth, soaking into his infamous beard. He smiled wide, baring his bloodstained teeth before coming at me.

It all felt like a recurring nightmare. Only a day had passed since my fight with Pan. The only difference tonight was my opponent. But Teach had overestimated his odds. My men had gathered around the deck to watch the spectacle. Smee stood at the center, leaving the fight to me, but I knew he had my back. If I couldn't manage to defeat him with one hand, they would finish the job for me.

I wanted to end this now, but his words plagued me. The idea of him with Katherine clouded my judgment. I couldn't trust anything that fucker said, and yet an uneasy panic took up residence in my gut. Nothing was right about this moment. Visions of his hands on her consumed my every thought. Leaving me exposed and he exploited it with a vicious right hook, landing squarely on my jaw. The impact made my teeth rattle. The silver tang of blood filled my mouth. Any normal man, especially one with my affliction, would have alarm bells signaling impending doom, but for me, it only fueled the fire.

I charged him again, the two of us falling as the deck pitched and rolled beneath us. We grappled on the floorboards, each of us twisting and rolling in a desperate attempt to gain the upper hand. Blow for blow, we traded punches. Though I felt the impact, pain seemed to be a distant notion. The only thing that registered was the need to make Teach pay. Pay for the loss of my hand, for corrupting my soul, for whatever he'd done to Katherine. Fury raged inside me, knowing that she'd been in his hands the whole time I'd been searching for her. It hadn't taken long for him to break her, and it was all my fault.

"Enough!" Katherine's command cut through the chaos.

My body stilled instantly as if I'd been cast in stone. The two of us were motionless, frozen in the midst of battle. We remained locked in place. The urge to fight drained from my body. Foreign magic crawled through my mind and altered my sentiments against my will. Only when the urge to fight had been smothered did the air around me calm, and my body became my own again. Teach and I untangled ourselves, and although I wanted him dead, I couldn't bring myself to raise arms against him.

I got to my feet and stared at Katherine. She stood tall, with her shoulders pulled back. A vacant expression on her face. The same stoic mask she'd worn the first day I'd seen her as she marched toward the witch's pyre. But it wasn't only her outward expression that drew my attention. A new necklace hung beside the locket she always wore. A tiny, corked vial. Its contents emanated an ethereal light. It was clear that the swirling contents contained magic of some sort. I'd wager it was the same magic that had violated my mind only moments before. The mystery of Katherine's disappearance continued to vex me. What had happened in the short time that I'd lost track of her? She was clearly different.

"Katherine, my love, I'm sorry for the way I've behaved. Please forgive me."

She closed her eyes, deep lines cutting across her brow before she met my gaze. Shadows danced within her clouded emerald eyes. What I saw there wasn't the soft, loving expression I'd grown accustomed to. It was harsh and menacing.

"James, I am no longer interested in your apologies." Her words were bitter, triggering a shiver that ran up my spine and settled in my chest.

"Can we talk about this in private? I know I have some explaining—"

"No, I'm not here to talk things over. I've only come to say goodbye."

"Goodbye? What are you talking about? We had a fight, but we still love each other. Goodbye is a word that doesn't exist between you and me," I said with a nervous laugh, trying to diffuse the intensity of the situation.

"James, don't make this harder than it needs to be. I'm leaving you. That's all there is to it."

It hit me like a punch in the gut. After all we'd been through, her words were devoid of emotion and completely callous as she dismissed the love we shared without a single tear. This wasn't my Katherine. The woman before me was a mere shell. My heart raced as the knot of anxiety expanded in my chest.

"You don't have to keep up this pretense. We have him outnumbered. He cannot hurt you again. I promise I'll make him suffer for what he's done to you."

I took a step toward her, reaching out. Only for her to recoil from me, taking a hasty step backward and clutching the railing of the ship.

"Don't touch me. You have to let me go."

"Katherine, I don't know what's happened, but we can figure this out. Let's go to our cabin. I'll have Teach thrown in the brig so we can talk undisturbed," I pleaded.

"Don't make me do this, James." She tore her eyes from mine, slamming them shut tightly as her face paled. She looked like she might be sick.

My anxiety catapulted me into full-blown panic. "What's wrong? What's he done to you?"

She stood silent for a moment, her eyes shut, clutching at the new necklace, the glowing light emanating from between her fingers. When she opened her eyes again and met mine, it was as if another person was looking back at me. Her emerald eyes had lost their luster, and a shadow of magic danced in the dark depths. Now, it was my turn to recoil.

"Your question is all wrong. You should be asking, what have *you done* to me? You're the one who's broken us."

"That's not true," I countered. "All I've ever done is love you." I was vaguely aware that we had an audience, but I didn't care. Everything felt surreal—like the balance of my happiness hung on the outcome of this moment.

A sickly-sweet laugh escaped her lips. "You don't love me. You don't even know what love is. I was nothing more than a useful tool and a warm place to put your cock."

My entire world was crumbling before my eyes. "I *do* love you. You know it's true. I love you, and you love me," I shouted, and it sounded like a command. I began to lose control of my emotions.

"When you love someone, you're supposed to put them

first. You're supposed to sacrifice your own needs for theirs," she paused for a moment, swallowing hard. "But I have never come first, have I, James? I'm second, and I always have been. Your true love is revenge."

This was it. The turning point. I'd always thought that Katherine supported my mission. That she wanted to see me get the vengeance I deserved. All the while, I'd missed the signs. Missed the fact that my quest for revenge was costing me the one person who truly loved me.

"Oh, Katherine. I am sorry. I never—"

"Stop. Stop that right now!" she cried, cutting off my apology. "You're not the hero here. Your soul is dark. It's corrupt. I can see it in your eyes. You told me once, and I should have believed you—you are the villain."

Her words struck home. My heart stuttered in my chest. In the heat of passion, I'd shown her my darkness. But she was the one who was supposed to see whatever remnants of light remained.

"I can change. I'll give it up. We can leave Neverland tonight." I swallowed back the lump in my throat. "I'll renounce my vendetta against Pan. I'll rearrange fate. I'll change everything that I have planned. I'll do it all for you."

She was shaking her head before I'd even finished my sentence. "All of it is a lie. You're lying to me," she shouted, her voice on the edge of hysteria.

"I'm not lying. I love you! I'm more sure of that than anything in my life. Can't you see it in my eyes? Can't you hear it in my voice?" I pleaded, my words quavering with the emotions I could no longer contain.

"What I hear is a desperate man. Poor James had a rough childhood, and somehow, the universe owes you something now? Grow the fuck up! You're just as much of a child as Peter Pan. *Everyone* has been wronged in some way. *You* are not special. You need to get over yourself and move on with your life like the rest of us, just like I am doing now. Stop playing the victim. Life isn't fair, and maybe me leaving you is exactly what needs to happen for you to realize that."

I tried to swallow my anger, to convince myself that she didn't mean what she was saying. She was trying to push me away, and it was working. My ego was flayed open. I had confided in her, told her all my deepest, darkest secrets, and she was weaponizing them against me.

"Kat, I—I don't understand—"

"This just isn't our time, James. This isn't the life where we get to love each other."

"I refuse to believe that. You know it isn't true."

"I needed you to need me. To put me first. But you couldn't. You're incapable of love."

A growl ripped from my lips. I wouldn't let this go any further. I refused to let her continue down this path. My demon took over. Rage filled the hole that was burrowing into my heart. "I won't let you leave me. I will chain you to my side until you come to your senses if I must."

"Yet more evidence that you are the villain in this story. After all I've been through, you'd take away my freedom?

For what? To ensure you can fuck me whenever you please? You would force a life upon me that I do not want?"

"So, what? You're going to choose him over me?" I asked, gesturing to Teach, who stood watching with a smug grin on his face. "He's treated you like property. Even if I'm as bad as you say, I'm still better than him."

"You can't tell me how to feel. At least with Edward, I know where I stand. I know what I'm getting myself into," she said adamantly. Her hands trembled for a moment before she crossed them over her chest. "I. Do. Not. Want. You. Anymore! You must let me go."

I sank to my knees, the wooden deck rising to meet me.

"No, Kat. Please." I had been reduced to begging. A deep despair wormed its way into my breaking heart, eating me alive.

"You're making a fool of yourself, James."

"Please, please. Don't leave me. We can make this work. I can be better. I can love you better. Please give me another chance." Tears fell freely, wetting my cheeks, and I did not care that my men were witnessing me fall apart. The rest of the world had fallen away. Right now, it was only Katherine and me.

"I can't. My heart can't take it anymore. It has to end here."

"What about mine? You're ripping *my heart* out."

Katherine ignored me. Fishing into the folds of her dress, she pulled out the Heart of the Divine. The flawless ruby glinted in the last vestiges of light as it sunk into a blood-red sunset.

"It doesn't matter." She shook her head. "Your heart is empty. There is no love there. It's empty, just like this ruby." She chucked the stone at me, the ruby landing solidly in my lap. A crack of thunder filled my ears and shook the air around us. All the pieces began to come together. Her curious words, the new relic around her neck. But my mind wouldn't allow me to believe that she would have meddled with such power. My fingers shook as I held the stone up to the light to confirm what I was trying so hard to deny. The core, which had once swirled with an ethereal power, was now a simple spectrum of crimson. The magic was gone.

The skies opened, and the smell of petrichor filled my nostrils. Rain poured down all around us. "Katherine, what have you done?" My hand trembled as I held the useless relic. My eyes lifted, settling on the glowing magic that was now tied around her neck.

"A parting gift," she said, fingering the delicate necklace. "The magic of the cosmos is the least I was owed for all that you've put me through. Edward, it's time." She motioned to Teach, and he sidled up to her, offering his arm. I winced as she wrapped her delicate fingers around him and reached up to kiss his cheek. "I think he finally understands where my loyalties lie. I'm done here. Take me away so I never have to lay eyes on him again." She turned to look at me one last time, her haunting emerald eyes piercing through me. "Goodbye, James." Her words dealt a death blow to my heart, and the useless organ stuttered and faltered in my chest until my vision spun. The pain was excruciating. I couldn't move. The shackles of fate tightened around me. Forcing me to watch as she snapped her fingers and shimmered out of existence with my enemy by her side.

The woman I thought I loved, no longer existed. My tears mixed with the pouring rain, soaking me to the core. I was numb to everything except the decay that was spreading within me. It felt as though a part of my soul was dying, and I mourned for the woman I'd lost.

Maybe she was right, and revenge was my one true love because my only solace at that moment was that she hadn't left me to become Pan's mother. Katherine had seen me for who I truly was—a broken man. A villain in my own story. One who was not worthy of redemption. I remained on my knees, defeated in every way possible. The Divine had forsaken me.

CHAPTER NINTEEN
-RIGHTEOUSNESS-
James

T hree days, that's how long I stayed locked in my cabin. Smee tried on several occasions to lure me out of isolation, but I'd have none of it. My entire world had shattered, and all I wanted was to be alone. I cried. I turned my room upside down. I pleaded with the Divine to send her back to me, and at the same time, I wanted her to pay for making me suffer. She never truly loved me. She couldn't have. She was fully aware that her abandonment would break me, and yet she did it without flinching. She never even shed a tear. The one person I trusted to never hurt me ripped my heart out and stomped on it.

I'd numbed myself with rum and tinkered with the various poisons left behind in Katherine's apothecary, secretly wishing they would end my suffering only to find no solace. The wretched bitch left nothing behind but a few harmless weeds and pain elixirs. Nary a toxin strong enough to snuff out the life force that insisted on pumping through my body. In my frustration, I made a promise to myself to continue my training and master the art of alchemy. There was an entire universe of useful plants and compounds at my fingertips. I didn't need Katherine anymore. I didn't need anyone anymore.

My life was nothing but a timeline of betrayal and hurt. Time and time again, I'd allowed people into my heart, only to have them leave me broken and bleeding alone. My parents, Peter, Edward, Henry, and Katherine, all of them, in one way or another, chipped away at my humanity, stealing bits and pieces of my very soul, leaving nothing behind but an empty husk. I was a shell of a man, and no one, ever again, could hurt me. My heart was gone, my soul hidden behind a wall of stone. The Divine broke me. They put me on this path of anguish. They do nothing without warrant. That's what Tiger Lily had said. If the Divine wanted a monster, a villainous counterpart, to balance the scales, then they succeeded. From now on, the only person I'd ever care for was myself.

"Captain," Smee's voice seemed small from behind the door. "It's been four days, sir. We have news. Please come out and take your rightful place as Captain of this ship."

I pondered for a moment. What news could they possibly have? Did I care?

"We have found something. I think you'll want to see it."

I cracked the door and winced as I peered out at Smee, the sun being altogether too bright for my mood. "What did you find?"

"Come out and see for yourself. The crew brought it back to the ship. I think you'll be most pleased. Besides, we can't keep it here. We need to… ahh… dispose of it quickly."

Now he had my interest. I closed the door and pulled on my breeches, fumbling with them as I struggled with my hook. Opening the door, I left behind the refuge of my cabin and emerged a new man.

"Show me this *thing* you found."

"Aye, Captain. It's on the main deck, and it's causing quite the stink. Prepare yourself; it's… pungent."

The crew huddled around the thing in question, their noses pinched. "What is it you found? Move out of the way." The smell was familiar—putrid, sickly sweet, rotting flesh. I'd smelled it countless times while sailing with Blackbeard. It's a scent one never forgets. "Move!" I ordered.

"Is it?" Cookson asked, looking at me as I stared in disbelief.

There on the deck in a pale, lifeless, bloated heap was none other than Edward Teach. "Where did you find him?"

"We found him tangled up in the rocks along the northern shoreline of the Viridianwood. Drowning, I suspect?"

There was no blood to be seen. His clothing appeared to be relatively intact. No evidence of stab wounds or gunshots. Nothing to indicate how he had died. He'd been reduced to nothing more than a foul-smelling lump of decaying flesh. A gift from the Divine, perhaps? Atonement for all they'd taken from me? Katherine had been right. I was always meant to be the villain, and the Divine was pleased that I'd finally realized my path in this life.

"Was he alone?" I braced myself for the answer. I hated Katherine, but I didn't want her dead. She deserved to suffer.

"Aye, Captain," Mason croaked. "She was nowhere to be found," he answered, getting straight to the point. He knew exactly what I had been asking.

"Good. Fuck her!" I growled. "I hope she spends her days alone and miserable."

"What should we do with him, Captain?" Cecco asked.

"Fetch me a jar. This bastard likes to elude death. I want his prying eyes."

Cookson took off, returning promptly with a small dirty jar. "Will this suffice?"

I reached down, digging my hook into his lifeless eyes, and ripped them from their sockets. He would never again look upon something belonging to me. I'd keep them locked away in a long-forgotten trunk. His eyes would see nothing but darkness for all eternity. I wiped my slimy hook on Cookson's sleeve. "Take his body to the shoreline of Three Pence Bay. Ram a stake through his arsehole and up his spine. Make sure his head stays on straight and display him upright as a warning to all who try to fuck with Captain James Hook and his crew. Together, we'll laugh as the never birds feast on his rotting flesh. The Divine is on our side. His death proves it. We are done playing nice."

Twenty-four hours had passed since we found Blackbeard dead and bloated. I decided to pay his corpse a visit. A moment, perhaps, to share a final word with him. I wasn't sure if I was seeking closure or maybe I needed to see that he was indeed still dead. Either way, I found myself headed to the shoreline of Three Pence Bay.

The crew had done a beautiful job with Edward's body. Like a macabre scarecrow, he hung slumped over in a gruesome display. It hadn't taken long for the never birds to find him. They had already begun pecking away at his rotting frame, making quick work of his abdomen. His intestines had spilled out, decorating the shoreline with a fragrant exhibition of viscera.

"Edward, old friend, now that we're alone, I have some words for you." I paused, giving his corpse a moment in case it decided to reanimate. Again. "You're just as bad as Peter. In fact, dare I say, I think you might actually be worse. Using people for your own gain, no matter the cost. Nothing was sacred to you, was it?"

I kicked at the stake, remembering the unspeakable things he'd done to Katherine, causing more of his innards to spill out of his bloated abdomen. "You didn't deserve her, you know. Katherine was too good for you. Hell, she was too good for *me*. Though I wish her a lifetime of heartache, I'm delighted to know she wasn't destined to spend a lifetime under your rule. May you rot in hell or whatever it is your belief offers in the afterlife." I spat on his remains and headed back to the *Jolly Roger*. It was time to move on from Blackbeard's tyranny once and for all. That life was over. Time to start a new era. Captain James Hook and his crew were about to reign chaos upon all of Neverland.

"CAPTAIN," Mullens approached with caution, "welcome back. I take it everything with the umm… body was to your liking?"

"Yes, the crew's done a marvelous job. Followed my instructions to the letter. Well done." I began to head back to my cabin when Mullens purposefully cleared his throat. "Don't waste my time. What is it you need?"

"The gnomes are here, sir. They are demanding access to the bow of the ship.

"Why are there gnomes on my ship?"

"They said you requested them?"

I had all but forgotten commissioning the gnomes to carve Katherine's likeness into the bow of the *Jolly Roger*. I had intended it to be a surprise. A symbol of my undying love for her. I made my way over to the bow, thinking of how I wanted to proceed.

"Rindle, good sir, we have a change in plan," I said as I approached the stout gnome waiting patiently on the forecastle deck. His warm smile faded quickly behind his beard.

"Do you not want the figurehead anymore, sir?"

"Oh, to the contrary. Keep everything as planned; only bare her breasts."

"Bare her breasts, sir?" He looked at me, confused.

"Exactly. I want all who look at her to see her for what she really is. Blackbeard's whore. Besides, women on ships are bad luck. Her bared breasts will appease Manann."

He looked utterly mortified at the request, but like any good artisan, he kept his opinions to himself. "We'll need the day to complete the project."

"Perfect. Smee! Gather the crew. We're going hunting."

"Aye, Captain."

"Starkey, man the ship till we return. See that Rindle and his crew get everything they need."

"Aye, Captain. What exactly are you hunting?"

"Crocodiles, Lost Boys, Peter Pan, I'm not picky."

"I heard him crowing this morning. Seemed to be off to the east, towards their camp. I'd start there."

Everything was falling into place. The Divine were smiling down on me. Clearly, I was on the right path. The path to righteousness. I had been made for villainy, and no one, ever again, would stand in my way. It was time to get revenge on Peter fucking Pan.

EPILOGUE
Captain James Hook
PRESENT DAY

I once said to Katherine, "Life is difficult and often shrouded in shadows. We must seek our darkness, revel in it, or we'll never know where to shine the light." If I had only known how much wisdom rested in those words.

My journey has never been an easy one. But I realize now that it was not meant to be, and I have been humbled through my suffering. It's molded me into the man I am today. I have seen countless sunsets and lived an unnatural number of lifetimes. Each came with a lesson. A piece of the puzzle leading me to salvation.

Love had its own role to play. Worming its way into my heart and forever upending my life. But as fate would have it, love is not without its thorns. A painful measure used to keep us always seeking for that one true match. Each fracture of the heart is a reminder that we must go on.

Katherine was my thorn. I reveled in her beauty, indulging in a kind of love that was nothing more than a fleeting fragrance, unseen, and yet profound. Though our time together was tumultuous, I truly believed I loved her. However, I tried to hold on too tightly to what wasn't mine to keep. I can still recall the sting of that prick. But I know now that we are built by those who break us. I have not seen Katherine since that fateful day nor heard a single whisper of her existence. It has taken me centuries to understand that I was forged anew in that heartbreak. That pain led me down my destined path and delivered me to my Darling girl. My other half.

In the end, love is either a blessing or a teacher. It enters our lives like a fierce and exhilarating tempest, leaving behind a landscape forever altered. True love makes you a better person, mends your broken pieces, and ultimately makes you whole again.

What I felt for Katherine wasn't founded in love but in need. They are both four-letter words, but they mean very different things. We needed each other for a time and ushered each other into our fated roles. She wasn't the one the Divine had created for me. We were never soul mates.

As I watch the rippling tides beneath the Neverland sky,

the stars winking their bygone secrets, I am grateful for the love that has touched my life, both its ecstasy and its agony. It has shown me the essence of what it means to be truly alive. Katherine may have broken my heart, but she was leading me to my destiny. It was a truly selfless gift. Though it took me many years to find forgiveness, it has brought peace to my soul. The Divine had a plan all along. I got my happily ever after, and it came to me through the hands of Peter Pan.

More From T.S. Kinley
The Neverland Chronicles

-Prequel-

-Volume I-

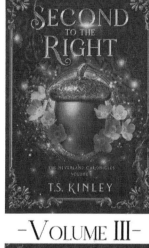

-Volume II-

-Volume III-

TSKinleyBooks.com

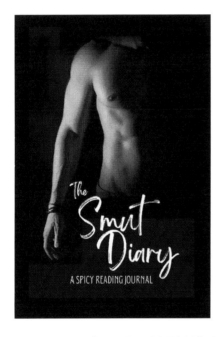

ABOUT THE AUTHOR

T. S. Kinley is a passion project created by two sisters with a shared obsession and vision. We came together with the dream of creating something beautiful, imaginative, and yes... SEXY. *Once Upon a Time...* it all began with sisterly gossip about erotica and romance novels. Our conversations quickly became fantasies about our own desires to author such work. We would muse how some day in a utopian future, our fantasy would become reality. Ultimately we decided rather than wait for the future to find us, we would create utopia ourselves. Using our love of books, natural gift of creativity, and some savvy study on publishing itself, the concept for our very first book was born. We started off as a Cosmetologist and an RN, and quickly developed into a dynamic writing team with a style that lends a unique perspective to our books.

If you haven't signed up already, please subscribe to the T.S. Kinley newsletter.

Receive exclusive sneak peeks on new releases, contests and other spicy content.

Visit www.TSKinleyBooks.com and sign up today!

Follow T.S. Kinley on social media. Let's be friends! Check out our Instagram, Facebook, Pinterest, and Tic Tok pages and get insights into the beautifully, complicated mind of not one, but two authors! You have questions, something you are dying to know about the amazing characters we've created? Join us online, we love to engage with our readers!

AUTHOR

LIKE WHAT YOU READ?

Did you enjoy your journey into the Neverland Chronicles?
Be a love and leave a review on Goodreads. While you are
there give us a follow.

Made in the USA
Columbia, SC
25 February 2025

8b429110-9d14-400e-ba78-b241ee6676fbR02